PRIDE AND PREJUDICE

By: Jane Austen

It is a truth universally acknowledged, that a single man in possession of a good fortune, must be in want of a wife.

"My dear Mr. Bennet," said his lady to him one day, "have you heard that Netherfield Park is let? It is taken by Mr. Bingley. A young man of large fortune from the north of England. You must visit him as soon as he comes."

"I see no occasion for that," replied Mr. Bennet.

"But consider your daughters."

"They have none of them much to recommend them. They are all silly and ignorant like other girls. But Lizzy has something more of quickness than her sisters."

"Mr. Bennet, how can you abuse your own children in such a way. You take delight in vexing me. You have no compassion on my poor nerves."

"Oh you mistake me my dear. I have a high respect

for your nerves. They are my old friends. I have heard you mention them in consideration these twenty years at least."

Mr. Bennet was so odd a mixture of quick parts, sarcastic humour, reserve, and caprice, that the experience of three and twenty years had been insufficient to make his wife understand his character. Her mind was less difficult to develop. She was a woman of mean understanding, little information, and uncertain temper. When she was discontented she fancied herself nervous. The business of her life was to get her daughters married; its solace was visiting and news.

Mr. Bennet was among the earliest of those who waited on Mr. Bingley. His wife and daughters had no knowledge of the visit until it was disclosed the following evening. The astonishment of the ladies was just what he wished. That of Mrs. Bennet perhaps surpassing the rest.

"Oh how good it was and you my dear Mr. Bennet. What an excellent father you have girls," said she.

The rest of the evening was spent in conjecturing how soon Mr. Bingley would return Mr. Bennet's visit and determining when they should ask him to dinner.

Mr. Bingley was meant to be at their next assembly and when his party entered the assembly room it consisted of Mr. Bingley, his two sisters, the husband of the eldest and another young man. Mr. Bingley was good looking and gentlemanlike; he had a pleasant countenance, and easy, unaffected manners. His sisters were fine women, with an air of decided fashion. His brother-in-law, Mr. Hurst, merely looked the gentleman; but his friend Mr. Darcy soon drew the attention of the room by his fine, tall person, handsome features, and noble mien; and the report which was in general circulation within five minutes after his entrance, of his having ten thousand a year. The gentlemen pronounced him to be a fine figure of a man, the ladies declared he was much handsomer than Bingley, and he was looked at with great admiration for about half the evening, till his manners gave a disgust which turned the tide of his popularity; for he was discovered to be proud.

Mr. Bingley had soon made himself acquainted with all the principal people in the room; he was lively and unreserved, danced every dance, was angry that the ball closed so early, and talked of giving one himself at Netherfield. Mr. Darcy danced only once with Mrs. Hurst and once with Miss Bingley, declined being introduced to any other lady, and spent the rest of the evening in walking about the room, speaking occasionally to one of his own party. His character was decided. He was the proudest, most disagreeable man in the world, and everybody hoped that he would never come there again.

Elizabeth Bennet had been obliged, by the scarcity of gentlemen, to sit down for two dances; and during part of that time, Mr. Darcy had been standing near enough for her to overhear a conversation between him and Mr. Bingley, who came from the dance for a few minutes, to press his friend to join it.

"Come, Darcy," said he, "I must have you dance. I hate to see you standing about by yourself in this stupid manner. You had much better dance."

"I certainly shall not. You know how I detest it, unless I am particularly acquainted with my partner. At such an assembly as this, it would be insupportable. Your sisters are engaged, and there is not another woman in the room, whom it would not be a punishment to me to stand up with."

"I would not be so fastidious as you are," cried Bingley, "for a kingdom! Upon my honour, I never met with so many pleasant girls in my life, as I have this evening; and there are several of them you see uncommonly pretty."

"You are dancing with the only handsome girl in the room," said Mr. Darcy, looking at Jane the eldest Miss Bennet.

"Oh! She is the most beautiful creature I ever beheld! But there is one of her sisters sitting down just behind you, who is very pretty, and I dare say, very agreeable. Do let me ask my partner to introduce you."

"Which do you mean?" and turning round, Darcy looked for a moment at Elizabeth, till catching her eye, he withdrew his own and coldly said, "She is tolerable; but not handsome enough to tempt me; and I am in no humour at present to give consequences to young ladies who are slighted by other men. You had better return to your partner and enjoy her smiles, for you are wasting your time with me."

Mr. Bingley followed his advice. Mr. Darcy walked off; and Elizabeth remained with no very cordial feelings towards him. She told the story however with great spirit among her friends; for she had a lively playful disposition, which delighted in anything ridiculous.

The evening altogether passed off pleasantly to the whole family. When Jane and Elizabeth were alone, the former, who had been cautious in her praise of Mr. Bingley before, expressed to her sister how very much she admired him.

"He is just what a young man ought to be," said she,

"sensible, good humoured, lively; and I never saw such happy manners! So much ease, with such perfect good breeding!"

"He is also handsome," replied Elizabeth, "which a young man ought likewise to be, if he possibly can. His character is thereby complete." She continued, "You like this man's sisters too, do you? Their manners are not equal to his."

"Certainly not; at first. But they are very pleasing women when you converse with them."

Elizabeth listened in silence, but was not convinced; their behaviour at the assembly had not been calculated to please in general; and with more quickness of observation and less pliancy of temper than her sister, and with judgment too unassailed by any attention to herself, she was very little disposed to approve them. They were in fact very fine ladies; not deficient in good humour when they were pleased, nor in the power of being agreeable where they chose it; but proud and conceited. They were rather handsome, had been educated in one of the first private seminaries in town, had a fortune of twenty thousand pounds, were in the habit of spending more than they ought, and of associating with people of rank; and were therefore in every respect entitled to think well of themselves, and meanly of others.

Mr. Bingley had inherited property to the amount of nearly an hundred thousand pounds from his father. His sisters were very anxious for his having an estate of his own; but though he was now established only as a tenant, Miss Bingley was by no means unwilling to preside at his table, nor was Mrs. Hurst, who married a man of more fashion than fortune, less disposed to consider her brother's house as her home when it suited her. Mr. Bingley had not been of age two years, when he was tempted by an accidental recommendation to look at Netherfield House. He did look at it and into it for half an hour, was pleased with the situation and the principal rooms, satisfied with what the owner said in its praise, and took it immediately.

Between him and Darcy there was a very steady friendship, in spite of a great opposition of character. Bingley was endeared to Darcy by the easiness, openness, ductility of his temper, though no disposition could offer a greater contrast to his own, and though with his own he never appeared dissatisfied. On the strength of Darcy's regard Bingley had the firmest reliance, and of his judgment the highest opinion. In understanding Darcy was the superior. Bingley was by no means deficient, but Darcy was clever and his manners, though well bred, were not inviting. In that respect his friend had greatly the advantage. Bingley was sure of being liked wherever he appeared, Darcy was continually giving offence.

Within a short walk of Longbourn lived a family with whom the Bennets were particularly intimate. Sir William Lucas was by nature inoffensive, friendly and obliging.

Lady Lucas was a very good kind of woman, not too clever to be a valuable neighbour to Mrs. Bennet. They had several children. The eldest of them, a sensible, intelligent young woman, about twenty-seven, was

Elizabeth's intimate friend.

That the Miss Lucases and the Miss Bennets should meet to talk over a ball was absolutely necessary; and the morning after the assembly brought the former to Longbourn to hear and to communicate.

The ladies of Longbourn soon waited on those of Netherfield. The visit was returned in due form. Jane Bennet's pleasing manners grew on the good will of Mrs. Hurst and Miss Bingley and though the mother was found to be intolerable, and the youngest sisters not worth speaking to, a wish of being better acquainted with them was expressed towards the two eldest Bennet daughters by Jane. This attention was received with the greatest pleasure but Elizabeth still saw superciliousness in their treatment of everybody, hardly accepting even her sister and could not like them. Though their kindness to Jane, such as it was, had a value as arising in all probability from the influence of their brother's admiration. It was generally evident wherever they met, that he did admire Jane and to her, it was equally evident that Jane's yielding to the preference with which she had begun to entertain for him from the first, and was in a way to be very much in love.

But Elizabeth considered with pleasure that it was not likely to be discovered by the world in general since Jane united with great strength of feeling, a composure of temper and a uniform cheerfulness of manner, which would guard her from the suspicions of the impertinent. She mentioned this to her friend Charlotte Lucas.

"It may perhaps be pleasant," replied Charlotte, "to be able to impose on the public in such a case; but it is sometimes a disadvantage to be so very guarded. In nine cases out of ten, a woman had better show more affection than she feels. Bingley likes your sister undoubtedly; but he may never do more than like her, if she doesn't help him on."

"But she does help him on, as much as her nature will allow. If I can perceive her regard for him, he must be a simpleton indeed not to discover it too."

"Ah, remember, Eliza, that he does not know Jane's disposition as you do."

"She is not acting by design," said Elizabeth, "as yet she cannot even be certain of the degree of her own regard."

"Well," said Charlotte, "I wish Jane's success with all my heart."

Occupied in observing Mr. Bingley's attentions to her sister, Elizabeth was far from suspecting that she was herself becoming an object of some interest in the eyes of his friend. Mr. Darcy had at first scarcely allowed her to be pretty; he had looked at her without admiration at the ball; and when they next met, he looked at her only to criticise. But no sooner had he made it clear to himself and his friends that she had hardly a good feature in her face, than he began to find it was rendered uncommonly intelligent by the beautiful expression of her dark eyes. To this discovery succeeded some others equally mortifying. Though he had detected with a critical eye more than one failure of perfect symmetry in her form, he was forced to acknowledge her figure to be light and pleasing; and in spite of his asserting that her manners were not those of the fashionable world, he was caught by their easy playfulness. Of this Elizabeth was perfectly unaware. To her he was only the man who made himself agreeable no where, and who had not thought her handsome enough to dance with.

He was thinking of her with some complacency, when thus accosted by Miss Bingley,

"I can guess the subject of your reverie."

"I should imagine not."

"You are considering how insupportable it would be to pass many evenings in this manner."

"Your conjecture is totally wrong, I assure you. My mind was more agreeably engaged. I have been meditating on the very great pleasure which a pair of fine eyes in the face of a pretty woman can bestow."

Miss Bingley immediately fixed her eyes on his face, and desired he would tell her what lady had the credit of inspiring such reflections. Mr. Darcy replied with great intrepidity, "Miss Elizabeth Bennet."

"Miss Elizabeth Bennet!" repeated Miss Bingley. "I am all astonishment. How long has she been such a favourite? And pray when am I to wish you joy?"

"That is exactly the question which I expected you to ask. A lady's imagination is very rapid; it jumps from admiration to love, from love to matrimony in a moment. I knew you would be wishing me joy."

"Nay, if you are so serious about it, I shall consider the matter as absolutely settled. You will have a charming mother-in-law, indeed, and of course she will always be at Pemberley with you."

He listened to her with perfect indifference, while she chose to entertain herself in this manner, and as his composure convinced her that all was safe, her wit flowed long.

The village of Longbourn was only one mile from Meryton; a most convenient distance for the young ladies, who were usually tempted thither three or four times a week, to pay their duty to their aunt. The two youngest of the Bennet family, Catherine and Lydia, were particularly frequent in these attentions; their minds were more vacant than their sisters', and when nothing better offered, a walk to Meryton was necessary to amuse their morning hours and furnish conversation for the evening. At present, they were well supplied with news and happiness by the recent arrival of a militia regiment in the neighbourhood.

Their visits to Mrs. Philips were now productive of the most interesting intelligence. Every day added something to their knowledge of the officers' names and connections.

After listening one morning to their effusions on this subject, Mr. Bennet coolly observed.

"From all that I can collect by your manner of talking, you must be two of the silliest girls in the country."

Mrs. Bennet was prevented replying by the entrance of a footman with a note for Miss Bennet. It came from

Netherfield.

"It's from Miss Bingley," said Jane, and then read it aloud.

"My Dear Friend,

If you are not so compassionate as to dine today with Louisa and me, we shall be in danger of hating each other for the rest of our lives, for a whole day's thte-a-thte between two women can never end without a quarrel. Come as soon as you can on the receipt of this. My brother and the gentlemen are to dine with the officers. Yours ever,

Caroline Bingley."

The following morning breakfast was scarcely over when a servant from Netherfield brought the following note for Elizabeth:

"My Dearest Lizzy,

"I find myself very unwell this morning, which, I suppose, is to be imputed to my getting wet through yesterday. My kind friends will not hear of my returning home till I am better. They insist also on my seeing Mr. Jones -- therefore do not be alarmed if you would hear of his having been to me -- and excepting a sore-throat and head-ache there is nothing much the matter with me.

Yours, Jane."

Elizabeth, feeling really anxious, was determined to go to Jane, though the carriage was not to be had; and as she was no horse-woman, walking was her only alternative.

"We will go as far as Meryton with you," said Catherine and Lydia. Elizabeth accepted their company, and the three young ladies set off together.

In Meryton they parted; the two youngest repaired to the lodgings of one of the officers' wives, and Elizabeth continued her walk alone, crossing field after field at a quick pace, jumping over stiles and springing over puddles with impatient activity, and finding herself at last within view of the house, with weary ankles, dirty stockings, and a face glowing with the warmth of exercise.

She was shown in to the breakfast-parlour, where all but Jane were assembled, and where her appearance created a great deal of surprise. That she should have walked three miles so early in the day, in such dirty weather, and by herself, was almost incredible to Mrs. Hurst and Miss Bingley; and Elizabeth was convinced that they held her in contempt for it. She was received, however, very politely by them; and in their brother's manners there was something better than politeness; there was good humour and kindness. Mr. Darcy said very little, and Mr. Hurst nothing at all. The former was divided between admiration of the brilliancy which exercise had given to her complexion, and doubt as to the occasion's justifying her coming so far alone. The latter was thinking only of his breakfast.

Jane's enquiries after her sister were not very favourably answered. Miss Bennet had slept ill, and though up, was very feverish and not well enough to leave her room. Elizabeth was glad to be taken to her immediately. The apothecary came and having examined his patient said that she had caught a violent cold, advised her to return to bed and promised her some draughts. The advice was followed readily for the feverish symptoms increased and her head ached acutely.

When the clock struck three, Elizabeth felt that she must go, but Jane testified such concern in parting with her, that Miss Bingley was obliged to offer an invitation to remain at Netherfield. Elizabeth most thankfully consented and a servant was dispatched to Longbourn to acquaint the family with her stay, and bring back a supply of clothes.

At five o'clock the two ladies retired to dress, and at half past six Elizabeth was summoned to dinner. When dinner was over she returned directly to Jane and Miss Bingley began abusing her as soon as she was out of the room. Her manners were pronounced to be very bad indeed. A mixture of pride and impertinence and she had no conversation, no style, no taste, no beauty. Mrs. Hurst thought the same, and added.

"She has nothing, in short, to recommend her, but being an excellent walker. I shall never forget her appearance this morning. She really looked almost wild."

"She did indeed, Louisa. I could hardly keep my countenance. Very nonsensical to come at all! Why must she be scampering about the country, because her sister has a cold? Her hair so untidy, so blowzy!"

"Yes, and her petticoat; I hope you saw her petticoat, six inches deep in mud, I am absolutely certain; and the gown which had been let down to hide it, not doing its office."

"Your picture may be very exact, Louisa," said Bingley; "but this is all lost upon me. I thought Miss Elizabeth Bennet looked remarkably well, when she came into the room this morning. Her dirty petticoat quite escaped my notice."

"You observed it, Mr. Darcy, I am sure," said Miss Bingley; "and I am inclined to think that you would not wish to see your own sister make such an exhibition."

"Certainly not."

"To walk three miles, or four miles, or five miles, or whatever it is, above her ankles in dirt, and alone! Quite alone! What could she mean by it? It seems to me to show an abominable sort of conceited independence, a most country town indifference to decorum."

"Its shows an affection for her sister that is very pleasing," said Bingley.

"I am afraid, Mr. Darcy," observed Miss Bingley, in a half whisper, "that this adventure has rather affected your admiration of her fine eyes."

"Not at all," he replied; "they were brightened by the exercise."

"Eliza Bennet," said Miss Bingley, "is one of those young ladies who seem to recommend themselves to the other sex by undervaluing their own, and with many man I dare say it succeeds. But in my opinion it's a paltry device, a very mean art."

"Undoubtedly," replied Darcy to whom this remark was

chiefly addressed, "there is a meanness in all the arts which ladies sometimes condescend to employ for captivation. Whatever bears affinity to cunning is despicable."

Miss Bingley was no so entirely satisfied with this reply as to continue the subject.

Elizabeth passed the chief of the night in her sister's room, and in the morning a note was dispatched to Longbourn. This was followed shortly by the arrival of Mrs. Bennet, accompanied by her two youngest girls. Mrs. Bennet was profuse in her acknowledgments and thanks for Miss Bingley's kindness. Elizabeth trembled lest her mother should be exposing herself again.

During the entire visit the two younger girls had been whispering together about the ball. Lydia with her assurance and easy manners was equal to remind Mr. Bingley of his promise. His answer was delightful to their mother's ear.

"I am perfectly ready, I assure you, to keep my engagement and when your sister is recovered, you shall if you please, name the very day of the ball."

Mrs. Bennet and her daughters then departed and Elizabeth returned instantly to Jane, leaving her own and her relation's behaviour to the remarks of the two ladies and Mr. Darcy; the latter of whom, however, could not be prevailed on to join in their censure of her, in spite of all Miss Bingley's witticisms on fine eyes.

Next evening after dinner, Elizabeth ran up to her sister and seeing her well guarded from cold attended her into the drawing-room where she was welcomed by her two friends with many professions of pleasure. When tea was over, Mr. Hurst had nothing to do but to stretch himself on one of the sofas and go to sleep. Darcy took up a book, Miss Bingley did the same and Mrs. Hurst, principally occupied in playing with her bracelets and rings joined now and then in her brother's conversation with Miss Jane Bennet.

Miss Bingley's attention was quite as much engaged in watching Mr. Darcy's progress through his book as in reading her own and she was perpetually either making some enquiry, or looking at his page. She could not win him however, to any conversation; he merely answered her question and read on. At length, quite exhausted by the attempt to be amused with her own book, which she had only chosen because it was the second volume of his, she gave a great yawn and said, "How pleasant it is to spend an evening in this way!"

No one made any reply. Miss Bingley soon afterwards got up and walked about the room. Her figure was elegant and she walked well. But Darcy, at whom it was all aimed, was still inflexibly studious. In the desperation of her feelings she resolved on one effort more and turning to Elizabeth said,

"Miss Eliza Bennet let me persuade you to follow my example and take a turn about the room. I assure you it is very refreshing after sitting so long in one attitude."

Elizabeth was surprised, but agreed to it immediately. Miss Bingley succeeded no less in the real object of her civility; Mr. Darcy looked up. He was as much awake to the novelty of attention in that quarter as Elizabeth herself could be, and unconsciously closed his book. He was directly invited to join their party, but he declined it, observing that he could imagine but two motives for their choosing to walk up and down the room together, with either of which motives his joining them would interfere.

Said he, "You either choose this method of passing the evening because you are in each other's confidence and have secret affairs to discuss, or because you are conscious that your figures appear to the greatest advantage in walking; in the first, I should be completely in your way; and if the second, I can admire you much better as I sit by the fire."

"Oh! Shocking!" cried Miss Bingley. "I never heard anything so abominable. How shall we punish him for such a speech?"

"Nothing so easy, if you have but the inclination," said Elizabeth.

"Tease him, laugh at him. Intimate as you are, you

must know how it is to be done."

"Oh, but upon my honour I do not. I do assure you that my intimacy has not yet taught me that."

"Mr. Darcy is not to be laughed at!" cried Elizabeth. "That's an uncommon advantage, and uncommon I hope it will continue, for it would be a great loss to me to have many such acquaintances. I dearly love a laugh."

"Miss Bingley," said Darcy, "has given me credit for more than can be. The wisest and best of men, nay, the wisest and best of their actions, may be rendered ridiculous by a person whose first object in life is a joke. But it has been the study of my life to avoid those weaknesses which often expose strong understanding to ridicule."

Elizabeth turned away to hide a smile.

"I am perfectly convinced by it that Mr. Darcy has no defect. He owns it himself without disguise."

"Do let us have a little music," cried Miss Bingley, tired of a conversation in which she had no share.

"Louisa, you will not mind my waking Mr. Hurst."

Her sister made not the smallest objection, and the piano-forte was opened, and Darcy, after a few moments recollection, was not sorry for it. He began to feel the danger of paying Elizabeth too much attention.

In consequence of an agreement between the sisters, Elizabeth wrote the next morning to her mother, to beg that the carriage might be sent for them. On Sunday, after morning service, the separation so agreeable to almost all, took place. Miss Bingley's civility to Elizabeth increased at last very rapidly as well as her affection for Jane, and when they parted, after showing the latter the pleasure it would always give her to see her either at Longbourn or Netherfield and embracing her most tenderly, she even shook hands with the former. Elizabeth took leave of the whole party in the liveliest spirits.

They were not welcomed home very cordially by their mother. Mrs. Bennet wondered at their coming, and thought them very wrong to give so much trouble, and was sure Jane would have caught cold again. But their father, though very laconic in his expressions of pleasure, was really glad to see them; he had felt their importance in the family circle. The evening conversation, when they were all assembled, had lost much of its animation, and almost all its sense, by the absence of Jane and Elizabeth.

"I hope, my dear," said Mr. Bennet to his wife, as they were at breakfast the next morning, "that you have ordered a good dinner today, because I have reason to expect an addition to our family party."

"Who do you mean, my dear?"

"The person of whom I speak, is a gentleman and a stranger. About a month ago I received this letter. It's from my cousin, Mr. Collins, who, when I am dead, may turn you all out of this house as soon as he pleases."

"Oh! my dear," cried his wife, "I cannot bear to hear that mentioned. Pray do not talk of that odious man. I do think it is the hardest thing in the world, that your estate should be entailed away from your own children; and I am sure if I had been you, I should have tried long ago to do something or other about it."

"It certainly is a most iniquitous affair," said Mr. Bennet, "and nothing can clear Mr. Collins from the guilt of inheriting Longbourn. But if you will listen to this letter, you may perhaps be a little softened by his manner of expressing himself."

"Dear Sir,

The disagreement subsisting between yourself and my late honoured father, always gave me much uneasiness, and since I have had the misfortune to lose him, I have frequently wished to heal the breach; but for some time I was kept back by my own doubts, fearing lest it might seem disrespectful to his memory for me to be on good terms with anyone, with whom it had always pleased him to be at variance. -- "There Mrs. Bennet." -- My mind however is now made up on the subject, for having received ordination at Easter, I have been so fortunate as to be distinguished by the patronage of the Right Honorable Lady Catherine de Bourgh, widow of Sir Lewis de Bourgh, whose bounty and beneficence has preferred me to the valuable rectory of this parish, where it shall be my earnest endeavour to demean myself with grateful respect towards her Ladyship, and be ever ready to perform those rites and ceremonies which are instituted by the Church of England. As a clergyman, moreover, I feel it my duty to promote and establish the blessing of peace in families within the reach of my influence; and on those grounds I flatter myself that my present overtures of goodwill are highly commendable, and that the circumstance of my being next in the entail of Longbourn estate, will be kindly overlooked on your side, and not lead you to reject the proffered olive branch. I cannot be otherwise than concerned at being the means of injuring your amiable daughters, and beg leave to apologize for it, as well as to assure you of my readiness to make every possible amends, - but of this hereafter. If you should have no objection to receive me into your house, I propose myself the satisfaction of waiting on you and your family, Monday, November 18th, by four o'clock, and shall probably trespass on your hospitality till the Saturday se'night following, which I can do without any inconvenience, as Lady Catherine is far from objecting to my occasional absence on a Sunday, provided that some other clergyman is engaged to do the duty of the day. I remain, dear sir, with respectful compliments to your lady and daughters, your well-wisher and friend,

William Collins."

"At four o'clock, therefore, we may expect this peace-making gentleman," said Mr. Bennet.

Mr. Collins was a tall, heavy looking young man of five and twenty. His air was grave and stately, and his manners were very formal. He had not been long seated before he complimented Mrs. Bennet on having so fine a family of daughters, said he had heard much of their beauty, but that, in this instance, fame had fallen short of the truth; and added, that he did not doubt her seeing them all in due time well disposed of in marriage.

They were not the only objects of Mr. Collins admiration. The hall, the dining-room and all its furniture were examined and praised. The dinner too in its turn was highly admired and he begged to know to which of his fair cousins, the excellence of its cookery was owing. But here he was set right by Mrs. Bennet, who assured him with some asperity that they were very well able to keep a good cook, and that her daughters had nothing to do in the kitchen. He begged pardon for having displeased her. In a softened tone she declared herself not at all offended; but he continued to apologize for about a quarter of an hour.

By tea time, Mr. Bennet was glad to take his guest into the drawing-room where Mr. Collins offered himself as his antagonist at backgammon.

Mr. Collins was not a sensible man and the deficiency of nature had been but little assisted by education or society. Having now a good house and very sufficient income, he intended to marry and seeking a reconciliation with the Longbourn family he had a wife in view as he meant to choose one of the daughters.

His plan did not vary on seeing them. Jane Bennet's lovely face confirmed his views. The next morning, however made an alteration; Mrs. Bennet felt it incumbent on her to hint that Jane was likely to be very soon engaged.

Mr. Collins had only to change from Jane to Elizabeth -- and it was soon done -- done while Mrs.

Bennet was stirring the fire.

Lydia's intention of walking to Meryton was not forgotten; every sister except Mary agreed to go with her; and Mr. Collins was to attend. As they entered Meryton, the attention of every young lady was soon caught by a young man whom they had never seen before of most gentlemanlike appearance, walking with an officer on the other side of the way. The officer was the very Mr. Denny, concerning whose return from London Lydia had come to inquire, and he bowed as they passed. Mr. Denny addressed them directly and entreated permission to introduce his friend, Mr. Wickham. The whole party was standing and talking together when Darcy and Bingley were seen riding down the street. On distinguishing the ladies of the group, the two gentlemen came directly towards them, and began the usual civilities. Mr. Darcy was beginning to determine not to fix his eyes on Elizabeth, when they were suddenly arrested by the sight of the stranger, and Elizabeth, happening to see the countenance of both as they looked at each other, was all astonishment at the effect of the meeting. Both changed colour, one looked white, the other red. What could be the meaning of it?

In another minute Mr. Bingley, without seeming to have noticed what passed, took leave and rode on with his friend.

Mrs. Philips was always glad to see her nieces, and the two eldest, from their recent absence, were particularly welcome. Some of the party were to dine with the Philipses the next day and their aunt promised to make her husband call on Mr. Wickham and give him an invitation also, if the family from Longbourn would come in the evening. This was agreed to and Mrs. Philips protested that they would have a nice, comfortable, noisy game of lottery tickets and a little bit of hot supper afterwards.

The coach conveyed Mr. Collins and his five cousins at a suitable hour to Meryton and the girls had the pleasure of hearing, as they entered the drawing-room that Mr. Wickham had accepted their uncle's invitation and was then in the house. Mr. Wickham was the happy man towards whom almost every female eye was turned and Elizabeth was the happy woman by whom he finally seated himself. He inquired how far Netherfield was from Meryton and after receiving her answer, asked in a hesitating manner how long Mr. Darcy had been staying there.

"About a month," said Elizabeth. "He is a man of very large property in Derbyshire, I understand."

"Yes," replied Wickham;- "his estate there is a noble one. A clear ten thousand per annum. You could not have met with a person more capable of giving you certain information on that head than myself - for I have been connected with his family in a particular manner from my infancy."

Elizabeth could not but look surprised.

"You may well be surprised, Miss Bennet, at such an assertion, after seeing, as you probably might, the very cold manner of our meeting yesterday. - Are you quite acquainted with Mr. Darcy?"

"As much as I ever wish to be," cried Elizabeth warmly, - "I have spent four days in the same house with him, and I think him very disagreeable."

"I have no right to give my opinion," said Wickham, "as to his being agreeable or otherwise. It is impossible for me to be impartial. But I believe your opinion of him would be in general astonishing."

"Upon my word, I say no more here than I might say in any house in the neighbourhood, except Netherfield. He is not at all liked in Hertfordshire."

"I cannot pretend to be sorry," said Wickham. "The world is blinded by his fortune and consequence, or frightened by his high and imposing manners, and sees him only as he chooses to be seen."

Wickham continued, "His father, Miss Bennet, the late Mr. Darcy was one of the best men that ever breathed and the truest friend I ever had and I can never be in company with this Mr. Darcy without being grieved to the soul, by a thousand tender recollections. His behaviour to myself has been scandalous; but I verily believe I could forgive him anything and everything, rather than his disappointing the hopes and disgracing the memory of his father."

He went on. "The church ought to have been my profession."

"Indeed!"

"Yes - the late Mr. Darcy bequeathed me the next presentation of the best living in his gift. He was my godfather, and excessively attached to me. I cannot do justice to his kindness. He meant to provide for me amply, and thought he had done it; but when the living fell, it was given elsewhere."

"Good heavens!" cried Elizabeth; "how could that be? - How could his will be disregarded? Why did you not seek legal redress?"

"There was such an informality in the terms of the bequest as to give me no hope from law. Certain it is, that the living became vacant two years ago, exactly as I was of an age to hold it, and that it was given to another man."

"This is quite shocking! Darcy deserves to be publicly disgraced."

"Some time or other he will be - but it shall not be by me."

"But what," Elizabeth said after pause, "what can have been his motive?"

"A thorough, determined dislike of me. Had the late Mr. Darcy liked me less, his son might have borne with me better."

"I had not thought Mr. Darcy to be as bad as this. I wonder that the very pride of this Mr. Darcy had not made him just to you."

"It's wonderful," replied Wickham, "for almost all his actions may be traced to pride."

After many pauses and many trials about the subjects, Mr. Wickham's attention was now caught by Mr. Collin's conversation and his reference to Lady Catherine de Bourgh. He asked Elizabeth whether her cousin were very intimately acquainted with the family of de Bourgh.

"Lady Catherine de Bourgh," she replied "has very lately given him a living."

"You know of course that Lady Catherine de Bourgh and Lady Anne Darcy were sisters and consequently that she is aunt to the present Mr. Darcy."

"No, indeed, I did not."

"Her daughter, Miss De Bourgh, will have a very large fortune, and it is believed that she and Darcy will unite the two estates."

This information made Elizabeth smile, as she thought of poor Miss Bingley. Vain indeed must be all her attentions, vain and useless her affection for Darcy's sister and her praise of himself, if he were already self-destined to another.

The prospect of the Netherfield ball was extremely agreeable to every female of the family. Mrs. Bennet chose to consider it as given in compliment to her eldest daughter and whilst particularly flattered by receiving the invitation from Mr. Bingley himself. Jane pictured to herself a happy evening in the society of her two friends, and the attentions of their brother; and Elizabeth thought with pleasure of dancing a great deal with Mr. Wickham and of seeing a confirmation of everything in Mr. Darcy's looks and behaviour. The happiness anticipated by Catherine and Lydia, depended less on any single event, or any particular person, for a ball was a ball.

Till Elizabeth entered the drawing-room at Netherfield and looked in vain for Mr. Wickham among the cluster of red coats there assembled, a doubt of his being present had never occurred to her. The absolute fact of his absence was pronounced by his friend Mr. Denny.

"I do not imagine his business would have called him away just now, if he had not wished to avoid a certain gentleman here," he said.

This part of his intelligence, assured Elizabeth that Darcy was answerable for Wickham's absence and she was resolved against any sort of conversation with him.

When the dancing recommenced however, Darcy

approached to claim her hand. At that moment Sir William Lucas appeared close to them meaning to pass through the set to the other side of the room; but on perceiving Mr. Darcy he stopped with a bow of superior courtesy to compliment him on his dancing and his partner.

"I have been most highly gratified indeed, my dear Sir. Such very superior dancing is not often seen. It is evident that you belong to the first circles. Allow me to say, however, that your fair partner does not disgrace you, and that I must hope to have this pleasure often repeated, especially when a certain desirable event, my dear Eliza, (glancing at her sister and Bingley), shall take place. What congratulations will then flow in! I appeal to Mr. Darcy: - let me not interrupt you, Sir. - You will not thank me for returning you from the bewitching converse of this young lady, whose bright eyes are also upbraiding me."

Sir William's allusion to his friend seemed to strike Darcy forcibly, and his eyes were directed with a serious expression towards Bingley and Jane who were dancing together.

Elizabeth and Darcy went on down the other dance and parted in silence. A short time later, Mr. Collins came up and told Elizabeth with great exultation that he had been so fortunate as to make a most important discovery.

"I have found out," he said, "by a singular accident that there is now in the room a near relation of my patroness."

"You are not going to introduce yourself to Mr. Darcy?"

"Indeed I am."

Elizabeth tried hard to dissuade him from such a scheme, but Mr. Collins listened to her with a determined of air of following his own inclination.

"My dear Miss Elizabeth, I have the highest opinion in the world of your excellent judgment in all matters within the scope of your understanding, but permit me to say that there must be a wide difference between the established forms of ceremony amongst the laity, and those which regulate the clergy. You must therefore allow me to follow the dictates of my conscience, which leads me to perform what I look on as a point of duty," and with a low bow he left her to attack Mr. Darcy whose reception of his advances she eagerly watched and whose astonishment at being so addressed was very evident.

When they sat down to supper Elizabeth considered it a most unlucky perverseness which placed Mr. Darcy near Mrs. Bennet and deeply was she vexed to find that her mother was talking freely, openly, and of nothing else but of her expectation that Jane would soon be married to Mr. Bingley.

In vain did Elizabeth endeavour to check the rapidity of her mother's words, or persuade her to describe her felicity in a less audible whisper; for to her inexpressible vexation, she could perceive that the chief of it was overheard by Darcy.

When supper was over, singing was talked of and Mary Bennet prepared to oblige the company. When Mary had finished her second song, Mr. Bennet said out aloud,

"That will do extremely well, child. You have

delighted us long enough."

To Elizabeth it appeared that her family made an agreement to expose themselves as much as they could during the evening, it would have been impossible for them to play their parts with more spirit, or finer success.

The Longbourn party were the last of all the company to depart; and by a manoeuvre of Mrs. Bennet, had to wait for their carriage a quarter of an hour after every body else was gone, which gave them time to see how heartily they were wished away by some of the Bingley family.

The next day opened a new scene at Longbourn. Mr. Collins made his declaration to Elizabeth in form.

"My reasons for marrying are first, that I think it a right thing for every clergyman in easy circumstances (like myself) to set the example of matrimony in his parish. Secondly, that I am convinced it will add very greatly to my happiness; and thirdly-which perhaps I ought to have mentioned earlier, that it is the particular advice and recommendation of the very noble lady whom I have the honour of calling patroness. Allow me, by the way to observe, my fair cousin, that I do not reckon the notice and kindness of Lady Catherine de Bourgh as among the least of the advantages in my power to offer. Your wit and vivacity, I think, must be acceptable to her especially when tempered with the silence and respect which her rank will inevitably excite. Thus much for my general intention in favour of matrimony; it remains to be told why my views were directed to Longbourn instead of my own neighbourhood, where I assure you there are many amiable young women. But the fact is, that being, as I am, to inherit this estate after the death of your honoured father, (who, however, may live many years longer), I could not satisfy myself without resolving to choose a wife from among his daughters, that the loss to them might be as little as possible, when the melancholy event takes place. This has been my motive, my fair cousin, and I flatter myself it will not sink me in your esteem. And now, nothing remains for me but to assure you in the most animated language of the violence of my affection. To fortune I am perfectly indifferent, and shall make no demand of that nature on your father, since I am well aware that it could not be complied with."

It was absolutely necessary to interrupt him now.

"You are too hasty, Sir," she cried. "You forget that I have made no answer. Let me do it without further loss of time. Accept my thanks for the compliment you are paying me. I am very sensible of the honour of your proposals, but it is impossible for me to do otherwise than decline them."

"You must give me leave to flatter myself, my dear cousin, that your refusal of my address is merely words of course. I shall choose to attribute it to your wish of increasing my love by suspense according to the usual practice of elegant females."

To such perseverance in wilful self-deception Elizabeth would make no reply, and immediately and in silence withdrew; determined, if he persisted in considering her repeated refusals as flattering encouragement, to apply to her father, whose negative might be uttered in such a manner as must be decisive, and whose behaviour at least could not be mistaken for the affection and coquetry of an elegant female.

While the family were in this confusion, Charlotte Lucas came to spend the day with them. She was met in the vestibule by Lydia, who flying to her, cried in a half whisper, "I am glad you are come, there is much fun here! -- What do you think has happened this morning? -- Mr. Collins has made an offer to Lizzy, and she will not have him."

Charlotte had hardly time to answer, before they were joined by Kitty, who came to tell the same news, and no sooner had they entered the breakfast-room where Mrs. Bennet was alone, than she likewise began on the subject, calling on Miss Lucas for her compassion, and entreating her to persuade her friend Lizzy to comply with the wishes of her family. "Oh, pray do, my dear Miss Lucas," she added in a melancholy tone, "for nobody is on my side, nobody takes part with me, I am cruelly used, nobody feels for my poor nerves."

Charlotte's reply was spared by the entrance of Jane and Elizabeth.

"Aye, there she comes," continued Mrs. Bennet, "looking as unconcerned as may be, and caring no more for us than if we were at York, provided she can have her own way. but I tell you what, Miss Lizzy, if you take it into your head to go on refusing every offer of marriage in this way, you will never get a husband at all -- and I am sure I do not know who is to maintain you when your father is dead."

Her daughters listened in silence to this effusion, sensible that any attempt to reason with or soothe her would only increase the irritation. She talked on, therefore, without interruption from any of them till they were joined by Mr. Collins.

"My dear Madam," said he, "let us be for ever silent on this point. My object has been to secure an amiable companion for myself with the due consideration for the advantage of all your family, and if my manner has been at all reprehensible, I here beg leave to apologize."

Next day a letter was delivered to Jane Bennet. It came from Netherfield and was opened immediately. The envelope contained a sheet of elegant, hot pressed paper, well covered with a lady's fair, flowing hand; and Elizabeth saw her sister's countenance change as she read it, and saw her dwelling intently on some particular passages. Jane recollected herself soon, and putting the letter away, tried to join with her usual cheerfulness in the general conversation; but Elizabeth felt an anxiety on the subject which drew off her attention even from Mr. Wickham; and no sooner had he and his companion taken leave, than a glance from Jane invited her to follow her up stairs. When they had gained their own room, Jane taking out the letter, said,

"This is from Caroline Bingley; what it contains, has surprised me a great deal. The whole party have left Netherfield by this time, and are on their way to London, and without any intention of coming back. I am sure now that Caroline neither expects nor wishes me to be her sister. That she is perfectly convinced of her brothers indifference and that if she suspects the natures of my feeling for him, she means, most kindly, to put me on my guard? Can there be any other opinion on the subject?"

"Yes, there can; for mine is totally different. -- Will you hear it?"

"Most willingly."

"You shall have it in a few words. Miss Bingley sees that her brother is in love with you, but wants him to marry Miss Darcy. She follows him to town in the hope of keeping him there, tries to persuade you that he doesn't care about you."

Jane shook her head.

"We are not rich enough, or grand enough for them," continued Elizabeth, "and she is the more anxious to get Miss Darcy for her brother, from the notion that when there has been one intermarriage, she may have less trouble in achieving a second."

They agreed that Mrs. Bennet should only hear of the departure of the Bingley family, without being alarmed on the score of the gentleman's conduct; but even this partial communication gave her a great deal of concern, and she bewailed it as exceedingly unlucky that the ladies should happen to go away, just as they were all getting so intimate together.

The Bennets were engaged to dine with the Lucases, and during the chief of the day, Miss Lucas was kind to Mr. Collins. Elizabeth took an opportunity of thanking her. Charlotte assured her friend of satisfaction in being useful. Charlotte's kindness extended farther than Elizabeth had any conception of; -- its object was to secure Mr. Collins' addresses. Appearances were favourable and it led Mr. Collins next morning to hasten to Lucas Lodge to throw himself at Charlotte's feet. His reception was of the most flattering kind and in as short a time as Mr. Collins' long speeches would allow, every thing was settled between them to the satisfaction of both. He earnestly entreated her to name the day that was to make him the happiest of men.

Sir William and Lady Lucas were speedily applied to for their consent; and it was bestowed with a most joyful alacrity. Charlotte herself was tolerably composed. Without thinking highly, either of men or of matrimony, marriage had always been her object.

As Mr. Collins was to begin his journey home too early on the morrow to see any of the Bennet family, the ceremony of leave-taking was performed when the ladies moved for the night; and Mrs. Bennet with great politeness and cordiality said how happy they should be to see him at Longbourn again, whenever his other engagements might allow him to visit them.

The next morning Charlotte Lucas called soon after breakfast and in a private conference with Elizabeth related the event of the day before.

"Engaged to Mr. Collins! My dear Charlotte, -- impossible!"

"I see what you are feeling," replied Charlotte, -- "you must be surprised, very much surprised, -- so lately as Mr. Collins was wishing to marry you. But when you have had time to think it all over, I hope you will be satisfied with what I have done. I am not romantic you know. I never was. I ask only a comfortable home; and considering Mr. Collins's character, connections, and situation in life, I am convinced that my chance of happiness with him is as fair as most people can boast on entering the marriage state."

Elizabeth quietly answered "Undoubtedly;" -- and after an awkward pause, they returned to the rest of the family. Charlotte did not stay much longer, and Elizabeth was then left to reflect on what she had heard.

Later that day Sir William Lucas himself appeared, sent by his daughter to announce her engagement to the family. Lydia, always unguarded and often uncivil, boisterously exclaimed.

"Good Lord! Sir William how can you tell such a story? Do not you know that Mr. Collins wants to marry

Lizzy?"

Elizabeth now put herself forward to confirm this account by mentioning her prior knowledge of it from Charlotte herself and endeavoured to put a stop to the exclamation of her mother and sisters by the earnestness of her congratulations to Sir William in which he was readily joined by Jane. And by making a variety of remarks on the happiness that might be expected from the match, the excellent character of Mr. Collins and the convenient distance of Hunsford from London.

Mrs. Bennet was in fact too much over powered to say a great deal while Sir William remained. But no sooner had he left than her feelings found a rapid vent. In the first place, she persisted in disbelieving the whole of the matter; secondly, she was very sure that Mr. Collins had been taken in; thirdly, she trusted they would never be happy together; and fourthly, that the match might be broken off. Two inferences, however, were plainly deduced from the whole; one, that Elizabeth was the real cause of all the mischief; and the other, that she herself had been barbarously used by them all; and on those two points she principally dwelt during the rest of the day. Nothing could console and nothing appease her. Nor did that day wear out her resentment. A week elapsed before she could see Elizabeth without scolding her, a month passed before she could speak to Sir William or Lady Lucas without being rude, and many months were gone before she could at all forgive their daughter.

Miss Bingley's letter arrived and put an end to doubt for Jane. The very first sentence conveyed the assurance of their being all settled in London for the winter and concluded with her brothers regret at not having had the time to pay his respects to his friends in Hertfordshire before he left.

Elizabeth, to whom Jane very soon communicated the chief of all this, heard it in silent indignation. To Caroline's assertion of her brother's being partial to Miss Darcy she paid no credit. That he was really fond of Jane, she doubted no more than she had ever done; and she said as much to her sister.

"You persist then in supposing his sister's influence on him?" Jane asked.

"Yes, in conjunction with his friend."

"I cannot believe it. Why should they try to influence him? They can only wish his happiness, and if he is attached to me, no other woman can secure it."

"Your first position is false. They may wish many things besides his happiness; they may wish his increase in wealth and consequence; they may wish him to marry a girl who has all the importance of money, great connections and pride."

"Do not distress me by the idea. I am not ashamed of being mistaken, or at least it is slight, it is nothing in comparison of what I should feel to thinking ill of him and his sisters. Let me take it in the best light, in the light in which it may be understood."

Elizabeth could not oppose such a wish; and from this time Mr. Bingley's name was scarcely ever mentioned between them.

Mr. Wickham's society was of material service in dispelling the gloom, which the late perverse occurrence had thrown on many of the Bennet family. They saw him often, and to his other recommendations was now added that of general unreserve. The whole of what Elizabeth had already heard, his claims on Mr. Darcy, and all that he had suffered from him, was now openly acknowledged and publicly canvassed; and everybody was pleased to think how much they had always disliked Mr. Darcy before they had known anything of the matter.

On the following Monday, Mrs. Bennet had the pleasure of receiving her brother and his wife, who came as usual to spend the Christmas at Longbourn. Mr. Gardiner was a sensible, gentlemanlike man, greatly superior to his sister as well by nature as by education. The Netherfield ladies would have had difficulty in believing that a man who lived by trade, and within view of his own warehouse, could have been so well bred and agreeable. Mrs. Gardiner, who was several years younger than Mrs. Bennet, was an amiable, intelligent, elegant woman, and a great favourite with all her Longbourn nieces.

The Gardiners stayed a week at Longbourn, and what with the Philipses, the Lucases and the officers there was not a day without its engagement. Mr. Wickham was sure to be one of the party and on these occasions Mrs. Gardiner, rendered suspicious of Elizabeth's warm commendations of him, narrowly observed them both. Without supposing them, from what she saw, to be very seriously in love, their preference of each other was plain enough to make her a little uneasy; and she resolved to speak to Elizabeth on the subject before she left Hertfordshire, and represented to her the imprudence of encouraging such an attachment.

"You're too sensible a girl, Lizzy, to fall in love merely because you are warned against it; and, therefore, I am not afraid of speaking openly. Seriously, I would have you be on your guard. Do not involve yourself, or endeavour to involve him in affection which the want of fortune would make so very imprudent. I have nothing to say against him; he is a most interesting young man; and if he had the fortune he ought to have, I should think you couldn't do better. But as it is -- you must not let your fancy run away with you. You have sense, and we all expect you to use it. Your father would depend on your resolution and good conduct."

"At present I am not in love with Mr. Wickham," Elizabeth replied. "No, I certainly am not. My father's opinion of me does me the greatest honour and I should be miserable to forfeit it. My father, however, is partial to Mr. Wickham. In short, my dear aunt, I should be very sorry to be the means of making any of you unhappy. All that I can promise you is not to be in a hurry. I will not be in a hurry to believe myself his first object. In short, I will do my best and I hope you are satisfied."

Her aunt assured her that she was and Elizabeth having thanked her with kindness of her hints, they parted.

Mr. Collins returned to Hertfordshire soon after it had been quitted by the Gardiners and Jane; who had accepted their invitation to stay with them in London.

The wedding took place; the bride and bridegroom set off for Kent and everybody had much to say on the subject. Elizabeth soon heard from her friend;

"My father and Maria are to come to me in March," wrote Charlotte, "and I hope you will consent to be one of the party."

Jane had already written a few lines to her sister to announce their safe arrival in London and when she wrote again, it was clear she could no longer be blind to Miss Bingley's inattention. After waiting at home every morning for a fortnight and inventing every evening a fresh excuse for her, the visitor did, at last appear, but the shortness of her stay and yet more, the alteration of her manner, would allow Jane to deceive herself no longer. The letter which she wrote on this occasion to her sister made it all too clear of what she felt.

Mrs. Gardiner, about this time, reminded Elizabeth of her promise concerning Wickham, and required information; and Elizabeth had such to send as might rather give it contentment to her aunt than to herself. His apparent partiality had subsided, his attentions were over, he was the admirer of someone else. The sudden acquisition of ten thousand pounds was the most remarkable charm of the young lady, to whom he was now rendering himself agreeable; but Elizabeth's vanity was satisfied with believing that she would have been his only choice, had fortune permitted.

March was to take Elizabeth to Hunsford to stay with Charlotte and Mr. Collins. Her travelling companions were Sir William Lucas and his daughter Maria a good humoured girl, but as empty headed as himself. Sir William had nothing to say that could be worth hearing, however, every object in the journey was new and interesting to Elizabeth.

At length the parsonage was discernible. The garden sloping to the road, the house standing in it, the green pales and the laurel hedge. Mr. Collins and Charlotte appeared at the door, and in a moment they were all out in a chaise rejoicing at the sight of each other. The evening was spent chiefly in talking over Hertfordshire news.

About the middle of the next day, Elizabeth observed Mr. Collins and Charlotte in earnest conversation with two ladies who had stopped in a low phaeton at the garden gates. Mr. Collins explained this by letting everyone know that Miss De Bourgh had come with an invitation to dine at Rosings the next day.

Mr. Collins' triumph in consequence of this invitation was complete. The power of displaying the grandeur of his patroness to his wondering visitors, and of letting them see her civility towards himself and his wife, was exactly what he had wished for.

From the entrance hall they had followed the servants through an ante-chamber to the room where Lady Catherine, her daughter and a Mrs. Jenkinson were sitting. Her Ladyship, with great condescension, arose to receive them; and as Charlotte had settled it with her husband that the office of introduction should be hers, it was performed in a proper manner, without any of those apologies and thanks which he would have thought necessary.

Lady Catherine was a tall, large woman, with strongly marked features, which might once have been handsome. Her air was not conciliating, nor was her manner of receiving them, such as to make her visitors forget their inferior rank.

The dinner was exceedingly handsome, and Lady Catherine seemed gratified by their excessive admiration.

When the ladies returned to the drawing-room, there was little to be done but to hear Lady Catherine talk. Elizabeth found that nothing was beneath this great lady's attention. She addressed a variety of questions to Elizabeth. How many sisters she had, whether they were older or younger than herself, whether any of them were likely to be married, whether they were handsome, where they had been educated, what carriage their father kept, and what had been her mother's maiden name? - Elizabeth felt all the impertinence of her questions, but answered them very composedly.

When Lady Catherine and her daughter had played cards as long as they chose, the tables were broke up, the carriage was offered to Mrs. Collins, gratefully accepted, and immediately ordered. The party then gathered round the fire to hear Lady Catherine determine what weather they were to have on the morrow. From these instructions they were summoned by the arrival of the coach, and with many, many speeches of thankfulness on Mr. Collins' part, they departed. As soon as they had driven from the door, Elizabeth was called on by her cousin, to give her opinion of all that she had seen at Rosings, which, for Charlotte's sake, she made more favourable than it really was. But her commendation, though costing her some trouble, could by no means satisfy Mr. Collins, and he was very soon obliged to take her Ladyship's praise into his own hands.

The first fortnight of Elizabeth's visit soon passed away. Easter was approaching and the week preceding it was to bring an addition to the family at Rosings. Elizabeth had heard, soon after her arrival, that Mr. Darcy was expected there in the course of a few weeks, and though there were not many of her acquaintance whom she did not prefer, his coming would furnish one comparatively new to look at in their Rosings parties.

His arrival was soon known at the Parsonage. Mr. Darcy had brought with him a Colonel Fitzwilliam, the younger son of his uncle. Elizabeth was sitting by herself one morning, when the door opened and to her great surprise, Mr. Darcy, and Mr. Darcy only, entered the room. He seemed astonished too, at finding her alone, and apologized for his intrusion by letting her know that he had understood all the ladies to be within.

"How very suddenly you all quitted Netherfield last November, Mr. Darcy! It must have been a most agreeable surprise to Mr. Bingley to see you all after him so soon; for, if I recollect right, he went but the day before. He and his sisters are well, I hope, when you left London?"

"Perfectly so -- I thank you."

She found she was to receive no other answer -- and, after a short pause, added,

"I think I have understood that Mr. Bingley has not much idea of ever returning to Netherfield again?"

"I have never heard him say so."

Elizabeth having nothing else to say, was now determined to leave the trouble of finding a subject to him.

He took the hint,

"Are you pleased with Kent?"

A short dialogue on the subject of the county ensued, on either side calm and concise -- and soon put an end to by the entrance of Charlotte and her sister, just returned from their walk. The tête-á-tête surprised them. Mr. Darcy related the mistake which had occasioned his intruding on Miss Bennet, and after sitting a few minutes longer without saying much to anybody, went away.

"What can be the meaning of this!" said Charlotte, as soon as he was gone. "My dear Eliza he must be in love with you, or he would never have called on us in this familiar way."

Indeed, why Mr. Darcy came so often to the Parsonage, is difficult to understand. Charlotte had once or twice suggested to Elizabeth the possibility of his being partial to her, but Elizabeth always laughed at the idea.

More than once did Elizabeth ramble within the Park. She was so engaged one day, when she saw Colonel Fitzwilliam was meeting her.

"I didn't know before that you ever walked this way," said she.

"I have been making a tour of the Park," he replied.

"Do you certainly leave Kent on Saturday?"

"Yes -- if Darcy doesn't put it off again. He arranges the business just as he pleases."

"I do not know anybody who seems more to enjoy the

power of doing what he likes than Mr. Darcy."

"He likes to have his own way, very well," replied Colonel Fitzwilliam, "but so we all do."

"I imagine your cousin brought you down with him chiefly for the sake of having somebody at his disposal. I wonder he does not marry to secure a lasting convenience of that kind. But, perhaps his sister does as well for the present, and, as she is under his sole care, he may do what he likes with her."

"No," said Colonel Fitzwilliam, "that is an advantage which he must divide with me. I am joined with him in the guardianship of Miss Darcy."

"Are you indeed?"

"She is a very great favourite of some ladies of my acquaintance, Mrs. Hurst and Miss Bingley. I think I have heard you say that you know them. There brother is a pleasant gentlemanlike man, he is a great friend of Darcy's."

"Oh, yes," said Elizabeth dryly, "Mr. Darcy is uncommonly kind to Mr. Bingley and takes a prodigious deal of care of him."

"Care of him! -- Yes, I have reason to think Bingley very much indebted to him."

"What is it you mean?"

"It is a circumstance which Darcy of course would not wish to be generally known, because if it were to get around to the lady's family it would be an unpleasant thing."

"You may depend upon my not mentioning it."

"What he told me was merely this; that he congratulated himself on having lately saved a friend from the inconvenience of a most imprudent marriage."

"Did Mr. Darcy give you his reason for this interference?"

"I understood that there were some very strong objections against the lady."

Elizabeth made no answer and walked on, her heart swelling with indignation. As she would not trust herself with an answer she therefore abruptly changed the conversation and talked on in different matters until they reached the Parsonage. The agitation and tears which this subject occasioned, brought on a headache; and it grew so much worse towards the evening that, added to her unwillingness to see Mr. Darcy, it determined her not to attend her cousins to Rosings, where they were engaged to drink tea.

Some time after they had gone, Elizabeth, as if intending to exasperate herself as much as possible against Mr. Darcy, chose for her employment the examination of all the letters which Jane had written to her since her being in Kent. It was some consolation to think that his visit to Rosings was to end on the day after the next, and a still greater, that in less than a fortnight, she should herself be with Jane again and enable to contribute to the recovery of her spirits by all that affection could do.

She was suddenly roused by the sign of the door bell. To her utter amazement she saw Mr. Darcy walk into the room. In a hurried manner he immediately began an inquiry after her health, imputing his visit to a wish of hearing that she were better. She answered him with cold civility. He sat down for a few minutes and then getting up walked about the room. Elizabeth was surprised, but said not a word. After a silence of several minutes he came towards her in an agitated manner and thus began.

"In vain have I struggled, it will not do. My feelings will not be repressed, you must allow me to tell you how ardently I admire and love you."

Elizabeth's astonishment was beyond expression. This he considered sufficient encouragement and the avowal of all that he had felt and had long felt for her immediately followed. There were feelings besides those of the heart to be detailed. She could not be insensible to the compliment of such a man's affection and aroused to resentment by his subsequent language, she lost all compassion in anger. He concluded with expressing his hope that he would now be rewarded by her acceptance of his hand.

The colour rose into her cheeks and she said,

"It is, I believe, the established mode to express a sense of obligation for the sentiments avowed. If I could feel gratitude I would now thank you, but I cannot. I have never desired your good opinion and you have certainly bestowed it most unwillingly. The feelings which you tell me have long prevented the acknowledgment of your regard, can have little difficulty in overcoming it after this explanation."

Mr. Darcy became pale with anger.

"And this is all the reply which I am to have the honour of expecting! I might, perhaps, wish to be informed why, with so little endeavour at civility, I am thus rejected."

"Had not my own feelings decided against you. Do you think that any consideration would tempt me to accept the man, who has been the means of ruining the happiness of a most beloved sister? Can you deny that you have done it?" she asked.

He replied, "I did everything in my power to separate my friend from your sister."

"It is not merely this affair," she continued, "on which my dislike is founded. Your character was unfolded in the recital which I received many months ago from Mr. Wickham."

"You take an eager interest in that gentleman's concerns," said Darcy.

"Who that knows what his misfortunes have been, can help feeling an interest in him?"

"His misfortunes!" repeated Darcy contemptuously.

"And of your infliction," cried Elizabeth with energy. "You have reduced him to his present state of poverty. You have deprived the best years of his life, of that independence which was no less his due than his dessert."

"And this," cried Darcy, "is your opinion of me! But perhaps these offences might have been overlooked, had not your pride been hurt by my honest confession of the scruples that had long prevented my forming the most serious design."

"You are mistaken, Mr. Darcy. You could not have

made me the offer of your hand in any possible way that would have tempted me to accept it."

His astonishment was obvious and he looked at her with an expression of mingled incredulity and mortification. She went on.

"From the very beginning of my acquaintance with you, your manners impressed me with the fullest belief of your arrogance, your conceit, and your selfish disdain of the feelings of others. I had not known you a month before I felt that you were the last man in the world whom I could ever be prevailed upon to marry."

"You have said quite enough, Madam. I perfectly comprehend your feelings and have now only to be ashamed of what my own have been. Forgive me for having taken up so much of your time and accept my best wishes for your health and happiness."

And with these words he hastily left the room.

The tumult of her mind was now painfully great. That she should receive an offer of marriage from Mr. Darcy! It was gratifying to have inspired unconsciously so strong an affection. But his abominable pride, his shameless avowal of what he had done with respect to Jane, his cruelty towards Mr. Wickham, soon overcame the pity which the consideration of his attachment had for the moment excited.

She continued in very agitating reflections till the sound of Lady Catherine's carriage made her feel how unequal she was to encounter Charlotte's observation and she hurried away to her room.

Elizabeth woke the next morning with the same thoughts and meditations which had at length closed her eyes. She could not yet recover from the surprise of what had happened; it was impossible to think of anything else. She resolved soon after breakfast to indulge herself in air and exercise. She was preceding directly to her favourite walk when the recollection of Mr. Darcy sometimes coming there stopped her, and instead of entering the Park, she turned up the lane which led her farther from the turnpike road. After walking two or three times along that part of the lane, she was tempted to stop at the gates and look into the Park. She was on the point of continuing her walk when she caught a glimpse of a gentleman within the sort of grove which edged the park; he was moving that way and fearful of it being Mr. Darcy, she was directly retreating. But the person who advanced, was now near enough to see her and stepping forward with eagerness, pronounced her name. She had turned away, but on hearing herself called, though in a voice which proved it to be Mr. Darcy, she moved again towards the gate. He had by that time reached it also, and holding out a letter, which she instinctively took, said with a look of haughty composure, "I have been walking in the grove some time in the hope of meeting you. Will you do me the honour of reading that letter?" -- And then with a slight bow, turned again into the plantation and was soon out of sight.

With no expectation of pleasure, but with the strongest curiosity, Elizabeth opened the letter, and to her still increasing wonder, perceived an envelope containing two sheets of letter paper, written quite through in a very close hand.

"Be not alarmed, Madam, on receiving this letter. I write without any intention of paining you, or humbling myself, by dwelling on wishes, which cannot be too soon forgotten. You must therefore pardon the freedom with which I demand your attention, but I demand it of your justice.

Two offences of a very different nature, and by no means of equal magnitude, you last night laid to my charge. The first mentioned was, that regardless of the sentiments of either, I had detached Mr. Bingley from your sister, -- and the other that I had, in defiance of various claims, in defiance of honour and humanity, blasted the prospects of Mr. Wickham. As to the first, I observed my friend's behaviour attentively and I could perceive that his partiality for Miss Bennet was beyond what I had ever witnessed in him. Your sister I also watched. Her look and manners were open, cheerful, and as engaging as ever but without any symptom of peculiar regard, and I remain convinced that though she received his attentions with pleasure, she did not invite them by any participation of sentiment. -- If you have not been mistaken here, I must have been in an error. With respect to that other more weighty accusation of having injured Mr. Wickham, I can only refute it by laying before you the whole of his connection with my family. My excellent father died about five years ago, and in his will, he particularly recommended to me to promote Wickham's advancement in the best manner that his profession might allow, and if he took orders, desired that a valuable family living might be his as soon as it became vacant. There was also a legacy of one thousand pounds. Mr. Wickham wrote to inform me that, having finally resolved against taking orders, he hoped I should not think it unreasonable for him to expect some more immediate pecuniary advantage, in lieu of the preferment. He had some intention of studying the law, he added. He resigned all claim to assistance in the church, and accepted in return three thousand pounds. For about three years I heard little of him; but on the decease of the incumbent of the living which had been designed for him, he applied to me again by letter for the presentation. His circumstances were exceedingly bad. He had found the law a most unprofitable study and was now absolutely resolved on being ordained. He trusted I could not have forgotten my revered father's intentions. You will hardly blame me for refusing to comply with this entreaty. His resentment was in proportion to the distress of his circumstances -- how he lived, I know not. But last summer, he was again most painfully obtruded on my notice. I must now mention a circumstance which I would wish to forget myself, but I feel no doubt for your secrecy. My sister was left to the guardianship of my mother's nephew, Colonel Fitzwilliam and myself. About a year ago, an establishment was found for her in London and she went with Mrs. Younge, the lady who presided over it to Ramsgate; and thither also went Mr. Wickham. There proved to have been a prior acquaintance between him and Mrs. Younge in whose character we were most unhappily deceived. My sister was persuaded to consent to an elopement. I am happy to add that I owed the knowledge of it to herself. Regard for my sister's credit and feelings prevented any public exposure to Mr. Wickham. Mr.

Wickham's chief object was, unquestionably my sister's fortune which is thirty thousand pounds, but I cannot help supposing that the hope of revenging himself on me was a strong inducement. This Madam is a faithful narrative of every event in which we have been concerned together. For the truth of everything here related I can appeal more particularly to the testimony of Colonel Fitzwilliam. I will only add, God bless you.

Fitzwilliam Darcy."

With amazement did Elizabeth first understand that he believed any apology to be in his power, and steadfastly was she persuaded that he could have no explanation to give. With a strong prejudice against everything he might say she began his recount of what happened at Netherfield. His belief in her sister's insensibility, she instantly resolved to be false. It was all pride and insolence.

But when this subject was succeeded by his account

of Mr. Wickham, her feelings were yet more acutely painful and more difficult of definition. The account of his connection with the Pemberley family was exactly what he had related himself. It was impossible not to feel that there was gross duplicity on one side or the other.

The extravagance and general profligacy which he scrupled not to lay at Mr. Wickham's charge, exceedingly shocked her. She tried to recollect some instance of goodness, some distinguished trait of integrity or benevolence, that might rescue him from the attacks of Mr. Darcy. But no such recollection befriended her. She could see him instantly before her, in every charm of air and address; but she could remember no more substantial good that the general approbation of the neighbourhood.

She perfectly remembered everything that had passed in conversation between Wickham and herself, in their first evening at Mrs. Philips'. She was now struck with the impropriety of such communication to a stranger. His attentions to Miss King were now the consequence of views solely and hatefully mercenary, and his behaviour to herself could now have had no tolerable motive.

She was absolutely ashamed of herself. Of neither Darcy nor Wickham could she think without feeling that she had been blind, partial, prejudiced, absurd.

Soon after her meeting with Mr. Darcy it was time for Elizabeth's visit to the Parsonage to draw to a close. Early in May Mr. Gardiner's chaise took the ladies first to Gracechurch Street and then, with Jane added to the party, to Hertfordshire. Their reception at home was most kind. Mr. Bennet rejoiced to see Jane in undiminished beauty and more than once during dinner did Mr. Bennet say voluntarily to Elizabeth, "I am glad you've come back Lizzy."

Their party in the dining room was large. For almost all the Lucases came to meet Maria and hear the news: and various were the subjects which occupied them; Lady Lucas was enquiring of Maria across the table, after the welfare and poultry of her elder daughter; Mrs. Bennet was doubly engaged, on one hand collecting an account of the present fashions from Jane, who sat some way below her, and on the other, retailing them all to the younger Miss Lucases; and Lydia, in a voice rather louder than any other person was talking to Elizabeth about the regiment.

"In a fortnight they will be gone from Meryton."

"Will they indeed," cried Elizabeth with the greatest satisfaction.

"They are going to be encamped near Brighton and I do so want Papa to take us all there for the summer."

Elizabeth's impatience to acquaint Jane with what had happened could no longer be overcome; and at length resolving to suppress every particular in which her sister was concerned, and preparing her to be surprised, she related to her the next morning the chief of the scene between Darcy and herself.

She then spoke of the letter repeating the whole of its contents as far as they concern George Wickham.

"I do not know when I have been more shocked," said

Jane, "Wickham so very bad. Almost past belief, and poor Mr. Darcy. Dear Lizzy, only consider what he must have suffered. Such a disappointment and with the knowledge of your ill opinion too. And having to relate such a thing about his sister, it really is too distressing. I am sure you must feel it so."

"Certainly. There is one point on which I want your advice. I want to be told whether I ought or ought not to make our acquaintances in general understand Wickham's character."

Jane paused a little and then replied, "Surely there can be no occasion for exposing him so dreadfully. What is your own opinion?"

"That it ought not to be attempted. Mr. Darcy has not authorized me to make his communication public. Wickham will soon be gone. At present I will say nothing about it."

"You're quite right. To have his errors made public might ruin him forever. He is now perhaps sorry for what he has done and anxious to re-establish a character. We must not make him desperate."

The tumult of Elizabeth's mind was allayed by this conversation. She had got rid of the secrets that had weighed on her for a fortnight. But there was still something lurking behind of which prudence forbade the disclosure. She dared not relate the other half of Mr. Darcy's letter, nor explain to her sister how sincerely she had been valued by his friend Bingley.

She was now, on being settled at home, at leisure to observe the real state of her sister's spirits. Jane was not happy. She still cherished a very tender affection for Bingley.

The first week of their return was soon gone. The second began. It was of the last of the regiment's stay in Meryton, and all the young ladies in the neighbourhood were drooping apace.

"Good Heavens! What is to become of us!" cried Lydia.

Their affectionate mother shared all their grief.

But the gloom of Lydia's prospect was shortly

cleared away; for she received an invitation from Mrs. Forster, the wife of the Colonel of the regiment, to accompany her to Brighton.

The rapture of Lydia on this occasion, the delight of Mrs. Bennet and the mortification of Kitty, are scarcely to be described. Wholly inattentive to her sister's feelings, Lydia flew about the house in reckless ecstasy. In vain did Elizabeth attempt to make her reasonable and detestable as such a step must make her were it known, she could not help secretly advising her father not to let her go.

"Oh, do not make yourself uneasy, my love," said Mr. Bennet. "Wherever you and Jane are known, you must be respected and valued, we shall have no peace at Longbourn if Lydia doesn't go to Brighton. Let her go then. Colonel Forster is a sensible man. She cannot grow many degrees worse without authorizing us to lock her up for the rest of her life."

Elizabeth was now to see Mr. Wickham for the last time. On the very last day of the regiment's remaining in Meryton, he dined with others of the officers at Longbourn; and so little was Elizabeth disposed to part from him in good humour, that on his making some enquiry as to the manner in which her time had passed at Hunsford, she mentioned Colonel Fitzwilliam's and Mr. Darcy's having both spent three weeks at Rosings.

"I think Mr. Darcy improves on acquaintance," she said.

"Indeed!" cried Wickham, with a look which did not escape her. "And pray how may I ask?" but checking himself, he added in a gayer tone, "Is it in address that he improves? Has he deigned to add ought of civility to his ordinary style? for I dare not hope," he continued in a lower and more serious tone, "that he is improved in essentials."

"Oh no!" said Elizabeth. "In essentials, I believe, he is very much what he ever was."

Wickham's alarm now appeared in a heightened complexion and agitated look. They parted at last with mutual civility and possibly a mutual desire of never meeting again.

When the party broke up, Lydia returned with Mrs. Forster to Meryton, from whence they were to set out for Brighton early the next morning. The separation between her and her family was noisy, rather than pathetic. Kitty was the only one who shed tears, but she did weep from vexation and envy.

When Elizabeth had stayed briefly with her aunt and uncle Gardiner on the way to Kent earlier that year to stay with Charlotte and Mr. Collins, she had been invited to accompany them on their tour to the lakes. She had joyfully accepted and the time fixed for the beginning of the tour was fast approaching. A fortnight only was wanting of it when a letter arrived from Mrs. Gardiner, which at once delayed its commencement and curtailed its extent. Mr. Gardiner must be in London again within a month, so they were obliged to give up the lakes and they were to go no farther northward that Derbyshire.

Four weeks were to pass before her uncle and aunt's

arrival at Longbourn, where they stayed only one night. They set off next morning with Elizabeth for Derbyshire and in particular the little town of Lambton, the scene of Mrs. Gardiner's former residence. Elizabeth found from her aunt that Pemberley was situated within five miles of Lambton.

"My love, should not you like to see a place of which you've heard so much?" said her aunt. "A place too, with which so many of your acquaintance are connected. Wickham passed all his youth there, you know."

Elizabeth was distressed. She felt she had no business at Pemberley, and was obliged to assume a disinclination for seeing it.

Mrs. Gardiner abused her stupidity. Elizabeth said no more-but her mind could not acquiesce. The possibility of meeting Mr. Darcy while viewing the place, instantly occurred. It would be dreadful!

When she retired that night, she asked the chambermaid whether Pemberley were not a fine place and whether the family were down for the summer. A most welcome negative followed the last question -- and her alarms were removed. When the subject was revived the next morning she could readily answer that she had not really any dislike to the scheme. To Pemberley, therefore, they were to go.

Pemberley house was a large, handsome, stone building standing well on rising ground and backed by a ridge of high woody hills. They were all of them warm in their admiration and at that moment Elizabeth felt that to be a mistress of Pemberley might be something.

On applying to see the place, they were admitted into the hall by the housekeeper a respectable looking elderly woman and Elizabeth longed to enquire whether her master were really absent but had not courage for it. At length however, the question was asked by her uncle. The housekeeper replied that he was, adding, "that we expect him tomorrow with a large party of friends."

On entering the dining-room, Elizabeth's aunt called

her to look at a picture. She approached, and saw the likeness of Mr. Wickham amongst several other miniatures. The housekeeper came forward and told them it was the picture of a young gentleman. The son of the late master's steward, who had been brought up by him at his own expense. -- "He is now gone into the army," she added, "-- afraid he has turned out very wild. And that," she said, pointing to another of the miniatures, "is my master -- and very like him. He's the best landlord and the best master that ever lived. Not like the wild young men now a days who think of nothing but themselves. There is not one of his tenants or servants but will give him a good name. Some people call him proud. I am sure I never saw anything of it to my fancy its only because he doesn't rattle away like other young men."

In what an amiable light does this place him, thought Elizabeth. As they walked across the lawn towards the river, Elizabeth turned back to look again. Her uncle and aunt stopped also and while the former was conjecturing as to the date of the building the owner suddenly himself came forward from the road which led behind it to the stables.

Their eyes instantly met and the cheeks of each were overspread with the deepest blush. Shortly recovering himself, he advanced towards the party, and spoke to Elizabeth, if not in terms of perfect composure, at least of perfect civility.

His resemblance to the picture they had just been examining was sufficient to assure the other two that they now saw Mr. Darcy. They stood a little aloof while he was talking to their niece, who, astonished and confused, scarcely dared lift her eyes to his face, and knew not what answers she returned to his civil enquiries after her family. Nor did he seem much more at ease. After a few more minutes of awkward conversation he asked her if she would do him the honour of introducing him to her friends. This was a stroke of civility for which she was quite unprepared and she could hardly suppress a smile at his now seeking the acquaintance of some of those very people against whom his pride had revolted.

What will be his surprise, thought she, when he knows who they are. He takes them for people of fashion. The introduction however, was immediately made and as she named their relationship to herself, she stole a sly look at him to see how he bore it and was not without the expectation of his decamping as fast as he could from such disgraceful companions. He sustained it however with fortitude and so far from going away, entered into conversation with Mr. Gardiner. Elizabeth could not but be pleased, that he should know she had some relations for whom there was no need to blush.

After walking some time through the grounds, Mrs. Gardiner, fatigued by the exercise of the morning, found Elizabeth's arm inadequate to her support and consequently preferred her husband's. Mr. Darcy took her place by her niece and they walked on together. Elizabeth observed that his arrival had been very unexpected, "for your housekeeper," she added, "informed us that you would certainly not be here till tomorrow."

He acknowledged the truth of it, "The rest of the party will join me early tomorrow," he continued. "There is one other person who particularly wishes to be known to you. Will you allow me, or do I ask too much to introduce my sister to your acquaintance during your stay at Lambton?"

Elizabeth was flattered and pleased and they parted on each side with the utmost politeness.

On the very morning after their own arrival at Lambton, Mr. Darcy brought his sister to visit and the formidable introduction took place. With astonishment did Elizabeth see that her new acquaintance was at least as much embarrassed as herself. She was exceedingly shy, and she found it difficult to obtain even a word from her beyond a monosyllable. Miss Darcy was tall, and on a larger scale than Elizabeth and though little more than sixteen, her figure was formed and her appearance womanly and graceful. There was sense and good humour in her face and her manners were perfectly unassuming and gentle.

They had not been long together, when Bingley's quick step was heard on the stairs, and in a moment he entered the room. He enquired, in a friendly, though general way, after her family and looked and spoke with the same good humoured ease that he had ever done.

In seeing Bingley, Elizabeth's thoughts naturally flew to her sister and, oh, how ardently did she long to know whether any of his were directed in a like manner. Certainly, though this might be imaginary, she could not be deceived as to his behaviour to Miss Darcy who had been set up as a rival of Jane, on this point she was soon satisfied.

It was not often that she could turn her eyes on Mr. Darcy himself, but whenever she did catch a glimpse, she saw an expression of general complaisance. Never had she seen him so desirous to please, so free from self-consequence or unbending reserve, as now. Their visitors stayed with them about half an hour and when they arose to depart, Mr. Darcy called on his sister to join him in expressing their wish of seeing Mr. and Mrs. Gardiner and Miss Bennet to dinner at Pemberley. Miss Darcy readily obeyed. Mrs. Gardiner, seeing in her husband who was fond of society, a perfect willingness to accept, the day after the next was fixed on.

That night Elizabeth lay awake two whole hours. Endeavouring to make out her feelings, she certainly didn't hate Darcy, no, hatred had vanished long ago and she had almost been ashamed of ever feeling a dislike against him that could be so called. Above all, above respect and esteem, there was a motive within her of good will which couldn't be overlooked. It was gratitute. Gratitude, not merely for having once loved her, but for loving her still well enough to forgive all the petulance and acrimony of her manner in rejecting him and all the unjust accusations accompanying her rejection. She respected, she esteemed, she was grateful to him, she felt a real interest in his welfare; and she only wanted to know how far she wished that welfare to depend upon herself, and how far it would be for the happiness of both that she should employ the power, which her fancy told her she still possessed, of bringing on the renewal of his addresses.

It had been settled in the evening, between the aunt and niece, that such a striking civility as Miss Darcy's, in coming to see them on the very day of her arrival at Pemberley, ought to be imitated. Consequently, they waited on her at Pemberley, the following morning.

On reaching the house they were shown through the hall into the saloon, where they were received by Miss Darcy, who was sitting there with Mrs. Hurst and Miss Bingley. Georgiana Darcy's reception of them was very civil; but attended with shyness and fear of doing wrong by Mrs. Hurst and Miss Bingley they were noticed only by a curtsy.

Elizabeth soon saw that she was herself closely watched by Miss Bingley and she couldn't speak a word especially to Miss Darcy without calling her attention. After sitting in this manner a quarter of an hour without hearing Miss Bingley's voice, Elizabeth received from her a cold enquiry after the health of her family. She answered with equal indifference and brevity and the other said no more.

Miss Darcy on her brother's entrance exerted herself to talk. Elizabeth saw that he was anxious for his sister and herself to get acquainted and forwarded, as much as possible, every attempt at conversation on either side. Miss Bingley saw all this likewise; and, in the imprudence of anger, took the first opportunity of saying, with sneering civility,

"Pray, Miss Eliza, are not the -- militia removed from Meryton? They must be a great loss to your family."

In Darcy's presence she dared not mention Wickham's name; but Elizabeth instantly comprehended that he was uppermost in her thoughts; and answered the question in a tolerably disengaged tone.

Their visit did not continue long after the question and answer above mentioned and while Mr. Darcy was attending them to their carriage, Miss Bingley was venting her feelings and criticisms on Elizabeth's person, behaviour, and dress. But Georgiana would not join her. Her brother's recommendation was enough to ensure her favour; his judgment could not err, and he had spoken in such terms of Elizabeth, as to leave Georgiana without the power of finding her otherwise the lovely and amiable.

"I remember when we first knew her in Hertfordshire," said Miss Bingley, when Darcy returned, "how amazed we all were to find that she was a reputed beauty and I particularly recollect your saying one night after they had been dining at Netherfield, -"she a beauty!" I should as soon call her mother a wit, but afterwards she seemed to improve on you and I believe you thought her rather pretty at one time."

"Yes," replied Darcy, who could contain himself no longer, "but that was only when I first knew her. For it is many months since I have considered her as one of the handsomest women of my acquaintance."

Mrs. Gardiner and Elizabeth talked of all that had

occurred, during their visit, as they returned, except what had particularly interested them both. Elizabeth was longing to know what Mrs. Gardiner thought of Darcy and Mrs. Gardiner would have been highly gratified by her niece's beginning the subject.

Elizabeth had been a good deal disappointed in not finding a letter from Jane, on their first arrival at Lambton; but on the third morning she received two letters at once, on one of which it was marked that it had been missent elsewhere. The one missent had been written five days ago. The beginning contained an account of all their little parties and engagements, but the latter half gave more important intelligence.

"Since writing the above, dearest Lizzy, something has occurred of a most unexpected and serious nature. An express came at twelve last night, just as we were all gone to bed from Colonel Forster, to inform us that Lydia was gone off to Scotland with Wickham. Imagine our surprise. To Kitty, however, it does not seem so wholly unexpected. I am very, very sorry. But I am willing to hope the best, and that his character has been misunderstood. Our poor mother is sadly grieved, my father bears it better. Colonel Forster gives us reason to expect him here soon. Lydia left a few lines for his wife, informing her of their intention. I must conclude for I cannot be long from my poor mother, I am afraid you will not be able to make it out, but I hardly know what I have written."

Elizabeth seized the other letter and opening it with the utmost impatience, read as follows:

"By this time, my dearest sister, you have received my hurried letter, I have bad news for you. Imprudent as a marriage between Mr. Wickham and our poor Lydia would be we are now anxious to be assured that it has taken place for there is too much reason to fear they are not gone to Scotland. Though Lydia's short letter to Mrs. Forster gave them to understand that they were going to Gretna Green, something was dropped by Mr. Denny expressing his belief that Wickham never intended to go there or to marry Lydia at all. All that is known is that they were seen to take the London road. After making every possible enquiry on that side of London, Colonel Forster came on into Hertfordshire, and broke his apprehensions to us in a manner most creditable. Our distress, my dear Lizzy, is very great. My father and mother believe the worst, but I cannot think so ill of him. I grieve to find, however, that Colonel Forster is not disposed to depend upon their marriage, he shook his head when I expressed my hopes, and said he feared Wickham was not a man to be trusted. Oh dearest Lizzy, I long for your return. I know my dear uncle and aunt so well that I am not afraid of requesting it, though I still have something more to ask of the former. My father is going to London with Colonel Forster instantly to try to discover her. What he means to do I am sure I know not. But his excessive distress will not allow him to pursue any measure in the best and safest way in such an exigence my uncle's advice and assistance would be everything in the world."

"Oh! where, where is my uncle?" cried Elizabeth,

darting from her seat. But as she reached the door it was opened by a servant and Mr. Darcy appeared. Her pale face and impetuous manner made him start, but before he could recover himself enough to speak, she hastily exclaimed, "I beg your pardon, but I must leave you. I must find Mr. Gardiner this moment, on business that cannot be delayed; I have not an instant to lose."

"Good God! what is the matter?" cried he, with more feeling than politeness, "I will not detain you a minute, but let me, or let the servant, go after Mr. and Mrs. Gardiner. You are not well enough; -- you cannot go yourself."

Calling back the servant, Elizabeth commissioned him to fetch his master and mistress instantly and then sat down, unable to support herself. Darcy could not refrain from saying in a tone of gentleness and commiseration, "Let me call your maid."

"No, no, I thank you, there is nothing the matter with me. I am only distressed by some dreadful news, which I have just received from Longbourn."

She burst into tears and for a few minutes could not speak another word. Darcy could only observe her in compassionate silence, at length she spoke again, "I have just had a letter from Jane, with such dreadful news. My youngest sister has thrown herself into the power of... of Mr. Wickham. They are gone off together from Brighton. She is lost forever."

"I am grieved, indeed," cried Darcy, "grieved, shocked. But is it certain, absolutely certain?"

"Oh yes! -- They left Brighton together on Sunday night, and were traced almost to London, but not beyond; they are certainly not gone to Scotland. My father is gone to London and Jane has written to beg my uncle's immediate assistance, but nothing can be done; I know very well that nothing can be done."

Darcy shook his head in silent acquiescence. His brow contracted; his air gloomy. Elizabeth soon observed and instantly understood it, her power was sinking, everything must sink under such a proof of family weakness. Such an assurance of the deepest disgrace. She could neither wonder nor condemn and never had she honestly felt that she could have loved him as now when all love must be in vain.

A pause of several minutes was broken by the voice of her companion, who in a manner which though it spoke compassion, spoke likewise restraint, said, "Would to heaven that any thing could be either said or done on my part, that might offer consolation to such distress. This unfortunate affair will, I fear, prevent my sister's having the pleasure of seeing you at Pemberley today."

"Oh, yes. Be so kind as to apologize for us to Miss Darcy. Say that urgent business calls us home immediately. Conceal the unhappy truth as long as it is possible. I know it cannot be long."

He readily assured her of his secrecy -- again expressed his sorrow for her distress, and leaving his compliments for her relations, with only one serious, parting, look, went away.

Mr. and Mrs. Gardiner had hurried back in alarm,

supposing by the servant's accounts, that their niece was taken suddenly ill; but satisfying them instantly on that head, Elizabeth eagerly communicated the cause of their summons. Though Lydia had never been a favourite with them, Mr. and Mrs. Gardiner could not but be deeply affected and Mr. Gardiner readily promised every assistance in his power.

Elizabeth, after all the misery of the morning, found herself in a shorter space of time than she could have supposed, seated in the carriage, and on the road to Longbourn.

They travelled as expeditiously as possible and sleeping one night on the road, reached Longbourn by dinner time the next day. When the carriage drove up to the door Elizabeth jumped out and hurried into the vestibule where Jane met her. She lost not a moment in asking whether anything had been heard of the fugitives, "Not yet," replied Jane, "but now that my dear uncle is come, I hope everything will be well."

"Is my father in town?"

"Yes. He went on Tuesday as I wrote you word."

"And have you heard from him often?"

"We've have only heard once to say that he arrived in safety."

"And my mother, how is she, how are you all?"

"My mother is tolerably well, I trust, though her spirits are greatly shaken. She does not yet leave her dressing-room. Mary and Kitty, thank heaven, are quite well."

"And you, how are you?" cried Elizabeth. "You look pale. How much you must have gone through."

Her sister, however, assured her of being perfectly well. Mrs. Bennet, to whose apartment they all repaired, after a few minutes of conversation together received them exactly as might be expected; with tears and lamentations of regret.

"Do not give way to useless alarm," said Mr. Gardiner, "as soon as I get to town I shall go to my brother, make him come home with me to Gracechurch street and then we may consult together as what is to be done."

In the afternoon, the two elder Miss Bennets were able to be for half an hour by themselves. "Tell me all and every thing about it, which I have not already heard," requested Elizabeth. "Give me further particulars. What did Colonel Forster say? Had they no apprehension of any thing before the elopement took place?"

"Colonel Forster did own that he had often suspected some partiality, especially on Lydia's side, but nothing to give him any alarm."

"And was Mr. Denny convinced that Wickham would not marry? Did he know of their intending to go off?"

"Denny would not give his real opinion about it. I am inclined to hope that he might have been misunderstood before."

"Not one of you entertained a doubt, I suppose, of their being really married?"

"How is it possible that such an idea should enter our brains? I felt a little fearful of my sister's happiness with him in marriage because I knew that his conduct had not always been quite right. My father and mother only felt how imprudent a match it must be. Kitty then owned, with a very natural triumph at knowing more than the rest of us, that in Lydia's last letter, she had prepared her for such a step. She had known, it seems, of their being in love with each other, many weeks."

"And did Colonel Forster appear to think ill of Wickham himself? Does he know his real character?"

"I must confess he did not speak well of Wickham as he formerly did. He believed him to be imprudent and extravagant. And it's now said, that he left Meryton greatly in debt."

The whole party were in hopes of a letter from Mr. Bennet the next morning but the post came in without bringing a single line from him. Mr. Gardiner had waited only for the letters before he set off, promising at parting to prevail on Mr. Bennet to return to Longbourn as soon as he could.

Mrs. Gardiner and the children were to remain in Hertfordshire a few days longer as the former thought her presence might be serviceable to her nieces. Their other aunt also visited them frequently and always, as she said, with the design of cheering and heartening them up, though as she never came without reporting some fresh instance of Wickham's extravagance or irregularity, she seldom went away without leaving them more dispirited than she found them.

All Meryton seemed striving to blacken the man, who, but three months before, had been almost an angel of light. He was declared to be in debt to every tradesman in the place, and his intrigues, all honoured with the title of seduction had been extended into every tradesman's family. Elizabeth though she did not credit above half of what was said, believed enough to make her former assurance of her sister's ruin still more certain; and even Jane, became almost hopeless.

Mr. Gardiner left Longbourn on Sunday; on Tuesday, his wife received a letter from him; it told them, that on his arrival, he had immediately found out his brother, and persuaded him to come to Gracechurch street. There was also a postscript to this effect.

"I have written to Colonel Forster to desire him to find out whether Wickham has any relations or connections who would be likely to know in what part of the town he has now concealed himself."

Every day at Longbourn was now a day of anxiety; but the most anxious part of each was when the post was expected.

Before they heard again from Mr. Gardiner, a letter arrived from a very different quarter, from Mr. Collins:

"My Dear Sir,

"I feel myself called upon, by our relationship, and by my situation in life, to condole with you on the grievous affliction you are now suffering under. Be assured, my dear Sir, that Mrs. Collins and myself sincerely symphathise with you, and all your respectable family, in your present distress.

The death of your daughter would have been a blessing in comparison of this. And it is the more to be lamented, because there is reason to suppose, that this licentiousness of behaviour in your daughter, has proceeded from a faulty degree of indulgence, though, at the same time, for the consolation of yourself and Mrs. Bennet, I am inclined to think that her own disposition must be naturally bad, or she could not be guilty of such an enormity, at so early an age. Lady Catherine and her daughter agree with me in apprehending that this false step in one daughter, will be injurious to the fortunes of all others, for who, as Lady Catherine herself condescendingly says, will connect themselves with such a family. Let me advise you then, my dear Sir, to console yourself as much as possible, to throw off your unworthy child from your affection for ever, and leave her to reap the fruits of her own heinous offence.

"I am, dear Sir, etc. etc."

Mr. Gardiner did not write again, till he had received an answer from Colonel Forster; and then he had nothing of a pleasant nature to send. Wickham had left gaming debts behind him to a very considerable amount. Colonel Forster believed that more than a thousand pounds would be necessary to clear his expenses at Brighton. He owed a good deal in the town, but his debts of honour were still more formidable.

Mr. Gardiner added in his letter, that they might expect to see their father at home on the following day, which was Saturday, and as Mrs. Gardiner began to wish to be at home, it was settled that she and her children should go to London, at the same time that Mr. Bennet came from it. The coach, therefore, took them the first stage of their journey and brought his master back to Longbourn.

When Mr. Bennet arrived, he had all the appearance

of his usual philosophical composure and it was some time before Elizabeth ventured to introduce the subject of Lydia. Then, on her briefly expressing her sorrow for what he must have endured, he replied,

"Say nothing of that. Who should suffer but myself. It has been my own doing and I ought to feel it."

"You must not be too severe upon yourself," replied Elizabeth.

"You may well warn me against such an evil. Human nature is so prone to fall into it! No, Lizzy, let me once in my life feel how much I have been to blame."

Two days after Mr. Bennet's return, an express came from   Mr.   Gardiner.

"My dear Brother,

"At last I am able to send you some tidings of my niece. Soon after you left me on Saturday, I was fortunate enough to find out in what part of London they were. I have seen them both. They are not married, nor can I find there was any intention of being so.

But, if you are willing to perform the engagements which I have ventured to make on your side, I hope it will not be long before they are. All that is required of you is, to assure to your daughter by settlement, her equal share of the five thousand pounds, secured among your children, after the decease of yourself and my sister. And, moreover, to enter into an engagement of allowing her, during your life, one hundred pounds per annum. You will easily comprehend from these particulars that Mr. Wickham's circumstances are not so hopeless as they are generally believed to be. I am happy to say there will be some little money even when all his debts are discharged to settle on my niece in addition to her own fortune. We have judged it best that my niece should be married from this house, of which I hope you will approve. She comes to us today. I shall write again as soon as anything more is determined on. Your's, etc.

"Edward Gardiner."

"Is it possible!" cried Elizabeth, "Can it be possible that he will marry her? The terms, I suppose must be complied with."

"Complied with! I am only ashamed of his asking so little."

"And they must marry! Yet he is such a man!"

"Yes, yes, yes, they must marry. There is nothing else to be done. But there are two things that I want very much to know: one is, how much money your uncle has laid down, to bring it about; and the other, how I am ever to pay him."

"Money! my uncle!" cried Jane, "what do you mean, Sir?"

"I mean, that no man in his senses, would marry Lydia on so slight a temptation as one hundred a year during my life, and fifty after I am gone."

"That is very true," said Elizabeth , "it must be my

uncle's doings! Oh, generous, good man. A small sum would not do all this."

"No," said her father, "Wickham's a fool, if he takes her with a farthing less than ten thousand pounds."

"Ten thousand pounds! Heaven forbid! How is half such a sum to be repaid?"

Mr. Bennet made no answer.

The girls went upstairs together. Mary and Kitty were both with Mrs. Bennet: one communication would, therefore, do for all. After a slight preparation for good news, the letter was read aloud. Mrs. Bennet could hardly contain herself. As soon as Jane had read Mr. Gardiner's hope of Lydia's being soon married, her joy burst forth, and every following sentence added to its exuberance. She was fidgety from alarm and vexation. To know that her daughter would be married was enough. She was disturbed by no fear for her felicity, nor humbled by any remembrance of her misconduct.

In terms of grateful acknowledgment for the kindness

of his brother, Mr. Bennet then delivered on paper his perfect approbation of the present arrangement. Mrs. Bennet found, however, with amazement and horror, that her husband would not advance a guinea to buy clothes for his daughter. He protested that she should receive from him no mark of affection whatever on the occasion. Mrs. Bennet could hardly comprehend it. She was more alive to the disgrace, which the want of new clothes must reflect on her daughter's nuptials, than to any sense of shame at her eloping and living with Wickham, a fortnight before they took place.

Elizabeth was now most heartily sorry that she had been led to make Mr. Darcy acquainted with fears for their sister. She had no fear of its spreading further, through this means. There were few people on whose secrecy she could have more confidently depended; but at the same time, there was no one whose knowledge of a sister's frailty would have mortified her so much. She began to comprehend that he was exactly the man, who in disposition and talents, would most suit her. By her ease and liveliness, his mind might have been softened, his manners improved, and from his judgment, information, and knowledge of the world, she must have received benefit of greater importance.

She was convinced that she could have been happy with him, when it was no longer likely that they should meet.

Mr. Gardiner soon wrote again to his brother. The principal purport of the letter was to inform him that Mr. Wickham had resolved on quitting the militia.

"It is Mr. Wickham's intention to go into the regulars; and among his former friends, there are still some who are able and willing to assist him in the army. He has the promise of an cornetcy in a regiment, now quartered in the north. I have written to Colonel Forster, to inform him of our present arrangements, and to request that he will satisfy the various creditors of Mr. Wickham in and near Brighton, with assurances of speedy payment. Will you give yourself the trouble of carrying similar assurances to his creditors in Meryton.

I understand from Mrs. Gardiner, that my niece is very desirous of seeing you all before she leaves the South. She is well, and begs to be dutifully remembered to you and her mother. -- Your's etc.

"E. Gardiner."

Mr. Bennet and his daughters saw all the advantages of the plan as clearly as Mr. Gardiner could do. But Mrs. Bennet, was not so well pleased with it. Lydia's being settled in the North, just when she had expected most pleasure and pride in her company, was a severe disappointment.

Her daughter's request, for such it might be considered, of being admitted into her family again, before she set off for the North, received at first an absolute negative from Mr. Bennet. But Jane and Elizabeth urged him to receive her and her husband at Longbourn as soon as they were married and when Mr. Bennet wrote again to his brother, therefore, he sent his permission for them to come.

Their sister's wedding day arrived. The carriage was

duly sent to meet them. The family were assembled in the breakfast room to receive them. Smiles decked the face of Mrs. Bennet, as the carriage drove up to the door; her husband looked impenetrably grave; her daughters alarmed, anxious, uneasy.

Lydia ran into the room. Her mother stepped forwards, embraced her, and welcomed her with rapture; gave her hand with an affectionate smile to Wickham, who followed his lady, and wished them both joy, with an alacrity which showed no doubt of their happiness.

Their reception for Mr. Bennet was not quite so cordial. The easy assurance of the young couple was enough to provoke him. Elizabeth was disgusted to see Lydia so unabashed, wild, noisy, and fearless. They seemed, each of them, to have the happiest memories in the world and Lydia led voluntarily to subjects which her sisters would not have alluded to for the world.

"Only to think of it being three months," she cried, "since I went away; I am sure I had no more idea of being married till I came back again! though I thought it would be very good fun if I was."

One morning soon after their arrival, as Lydia was sitting with her two elder sisters, she said to Elizabeth:

"Lizzy, I never gave you an account of my wedding, I believe. Are you not curious to hear how it was managed?"

"Not really," replied Elizabeth; "I think there cannot be too little said on the subject."

"La! You are so strange! But I must tell you how it went off. We were married, you know, at St. Clement's, because Wickham's lodgings were in that parish. And it was settled that we should all be there by eleven o'clock. Well, Monday morning came, and I was in such a fuss! I was so afraid you know that something would happen to put it off, and then I should have gone quite distracted. And there was my aunt, all the time I was dressing, preaching and talking away just as if she were reading a sermon. Oh by the by, you ought to understand that my uncle and aunt were horrid. Unpleasant all the time I was with them. I didn't once put my foot out of doors, though I was there a fortnight. Not a party, or scheme, or anything. We breakfasted at ten and just as the carriage came to the door, my uncle was called away on business. I was so frightened I didn't know what to do, for my uncle was to give me away. Luckily he came back again in ten minutes time and we all set out again. However, I recollected afterwards, that had he been prevented going, the wedding need not be put off for Mr. Darcy might have done as well."

"Mr. Darcy!" repeated Elizabeth in utter amazement.

"Oh yes! -- he was to come there with Wickham, you know. Gracious me. I quite forgot! I ought not to have said a word about it. It was to be such a secret!"

Elizabeth burning with curiosity was forced to put it out of her power to ask questions by running way. But to live in ignorance on such a point was impossible or at least it was impossible not to try for information. Hastily seizing a sheet of paper, she wrote a short letter to her aunt to request an explanation of what

Lydia had dropped, if it were compatible with the secrecy which had been intended.

Elizabeth had the satisfaction of receiving an answer to her letter as soon as she possibly could. Hurrying into the little copse, she sat down on one of the benches to read.

"My Dear Niece,

"I have just received you letter, and hastened to answer. On the very day of my coming home from Longbourn, your uncle had a most unexpected visitor. Mr. Darcy called and was shut up with him several hours. He came to tell your uncle that he had found out where your sister and Mr. Wickham were and that he had seen and talked with them both. Wickham repeatedly, Lydia once. He had been some days in town before he was able to discover them but he had something to direct his search. There is a lady it seems, a Mrs. Younge, who was sometime ago governess to

Miss Darcy and was dismissed from her charge. She then took a large house in Edwards Street and has since maintained herself by letting lodgings. This Mrs. Younge was, he knew, intimately acquainted with Wickham; and he went to her for intelligence of him. Wickham had indeed gone to her on their first arrival in London and had she been able to receive them into her house, they would have taken up their abode with her. At length, however, our kind friend procured the wished-for direction. He saw Wickham and afterwards insisted on seeing Lydia. He found Lydia absolutely resolved on remaining where she was. She would not hear of leaving Wickham. She was sure they would be married some time or other, and it did not much signify when. Since such were her feelings, it only remained, he thought, to secure and expedite a marriage, which, in his very first conversation with Wickham, he easily learnt, had never been his design. He confessed himself obliged to leave the regiment, on account of debts of honour. He meant to resign his commission immediately and had nothing to live on. He still cherished the hope of more effectually making his fortune by marriage in some other country. Under such circumstances however, he was not likely to be proof against the temptation of immediate relief. They met several times, for there was much to be discussed. Wickham, of course, wanted more than he could get; but at length was reduced to be reasonable. Everything being settled between them, Mr. Darcy called in Gracechurch-street and he and your uncle had a great deal of talk together. At last your uncle was forced to yield and instead of being allowed to be of use to his niece was forced to put up with only having the credit of it. But Lizzy, this must go no farther than yourself or Jane at the most. You know pretty well, I suppose, what has been done for the young people. His debts are to be paid, amounting I believe, to considerably more than a thousand pounds. Another thousand, in addition to her own being settled upon her and his commission purchased. The reason why all this was to be done by Darcy alone was that it was owing to him that his reserve and want of proper consideration, that Wickham's character had been so misunderstood and consequently that he had been received and noticed as he was. In spite of all this fine talking, my dear Lizzy, you may rest perfectly assured we gave him credit for another interest in the affair. After all was arranged, Mr. Darcy, as Lydia informed you, attended the wedding. He dined with us the next day and was to leave town again on Wednesday or Thursday. Will you be very angry with me, my dear Lizzy, if I take this opportunity of saying how much I like him. His behaviour to us has, in every respect, been as pleasing as when we were in Derbyshire. His understanding and opinions all please me; he wants nothing but a little more liveliness, and that, if he marry prudently, his wife may teach him. Pray forgive me if I have been very presuming, or at least do not punish me so far, as to exclude me from Pemberley. I shall never be quite happy till I have been all round the park. A low phaeton, with a nice little pair of ponies, would be the very thing. But I must write no more. The children have been wanting me this half hour. Your's, very sincerely,

"M. Gardiner."

The contents of this letter threw Elizabeth into a

flutter of spirits. Mr. Darcy had done all this for Lydia whom he could neither regard or esteem. Her heart did whisper, that he had done it for her. But it was a hope shortly checked by other considerations. For herself she was humbled but she was proud of him. Proud that in a course of compassion and honour, he had been able to get the better of himself. She was roused from her reflections by someone's approach. It was Wickham.

"I am afraid I interrupt you my dear sister?" said he.

"You certainly do," she replied with a smile, "but it does not follow that the interruption must be unwelcome."

"I find from our uncle and aunt that you have actually seen Pemberley?"

Elizabeth replied in the affirmative.

"You saw the old housekeeper I suppose? Poor Mrs. Reynolds, she was always very fond of me. But of course she didn't mention my name to you."

"Yes, she did."

"And what did she say?"

"That you were gone into the army, and she was afraid had-not turned out well. At such a distance as that, you know, things are strangely misrepresented."

"Certainly," he replied, biting his lips. Elizabeth hoped she'd silenced him; but he soon afterwards said,

"I was surprised to see Darcy in town last month. We passed each other several times. Did you see him while you were at Lambton? I thought I understood from the Gardiners that you had."

"Yes; he introduced us to his sister."

"And do you like her?"

"Very much."

"Oh, I have heard she is uncommonly improved within this year or two. Did you go to the village of Kympton?"

"I do not recollect that we did."

"I mention it because it is the living which I ought to have had. A most delightful place! -- Excellent Parsonage House! It would have suited me in every respect."

"How should you have liked making sermons?"

"Exceedingly well. The quiet, the retirement of such a life, would have answered all my ideas of happiness! But it was not to be. Did you ever hear Darcy mention the circumstance, when you were in Kent?"

"I have heard that it was left you conditionally only, and at the will of the present patron."

"Yes, there is something in that; I told you so from the first, you may remember."

"I did hear, too, that there was a time, when sermon-making was not so palatable to you as it seems to be at present."

They were now almost at the door of the house, and unwilling for her sister's sake, to provoke him, she said with a good-humoured smile,

"Come, Mr. Wickham, we are brother and sister you know. Do not let us quarrel about the past. In future, I hope we shall be always of one mind."

She held out her hand; he kissed it with affectionate gallantry, though he hardly knew how to look, and they entered the house.

The day of Lydia's departure soon came, and the loss of her daughter made Mrs. Bennet very dull for several days. But the spiritless condition which this event threw her into, was shortly relieved by an article of news, which then began to be in circulation. The housekeeper at Netherfield had received orders to prepare for the arrival of her master, who was coming down to shoot there for several weeks.

The subject which had been so warmly canvassed between their parents, about a twelvemonth ago, was now brought forward again.

"As soon as ever Mr. Bingley comes, my dear," said Mrs. Bennet, "you will wait on him of course."

"No, no, no. You forced me into visiting him last year, and it ended in nothing; I will not be sent on a fool's errand again."

"All I know is that it will be abominably rude if you do not wait on him. But that shan't prevent my asking him to dine here," replied Mrs. Bennet.

Mr. Bingley arrived at Netherfield. Mrs. Bennet counted the days that must intervene before her invitation could be sent; hopeless of seeing him before. But on the third morning after his arrival in Hertfordshire, she saw him from her dressing-room window, enter the paddock, and ride towards the house.

"There is a gentleman with him, mamma," said Kitty; "it looks like that man that used to be with him before. Mr. ...um, what's his name? That tall, proud man, who can it be?"

"Good gracious! Mr. Darcy! -- and so it does I vow. Well, any friend of Mr. Bingley's will always be welcome here to be sure, but I must say I hate the very sight of him."

Jane looked a little paler than usual. More sedate that Elizabeth had expected. On the gentlemen's appearing, her colour increased. Yet she received them with tolerable ease. Elizabeth said as little to either as civility would allow. She had ventured only one glance at Darcy. He looked as serious as usual; and she thought, more as he had been used to look in Hertfordshire, than as she had seen him at Pemberley. But, perhaps he could not, in her mother's presence, be what he was before her uncle and aunt. It was a painful, but not an improbable, conjecture.

Bingley was received by Mrs. Bennet with a degree of civility which made her two daughters ashamed especially when contrasted with the cold and ceremonious politeness of her curtsey and address to his friend.

Elizabeth was hurt and distressed to a most painful degree by a distinction so ill applied.

Darcy said scarcely anything and when occasionally unable to resist the impulse of curiosity, Elizabeth raised her eyes to his face, she as often found him looking at Jane, as at herself.

"Could I expect it otherwise!" said she to herself. "Yet why did he come?"

"It is a long time, Mr. Bingley, since you went away," said Mrs. Bennet.

He readily agreed to it.

"A great many changes have happened in the neighbourhood since you went away. Miss Lucas is married and settled. And one of my own daughters. You must have seen it in the papers, it was in the Times and the Courier, I know though it was not put in as it ought to be. It was only said, "Lately, George Wickham, Esq. to Miss Lydia Bennet," did you see it?"

Bingley replied that he had, and made his congratulations.

"His regiment is in the North, for I suppose you have heard of his being gone into the regulars. Thank Heavens! he has some friends, though perhaps not so many as he deserves."

Elizabeth, who knew this to be levelled at Mr. Darcy, was in such misery of shame, that she could hardly keep her seat.

"When you have killed all your own birds, Mr. Bingley," said her mother, "I beg you will come here, and shoot as many as you please, on Mr. Bennet's manor. I am sure he will save all the best of the coveys for you."

Elizabeth's misery increased.

"The first wish of my heart," said she to herself, "is never more to be in company with either of them. Let me never see either one or the other again!"

Yet the misery, for which years of happiness were to offer no compensation, received soon afterwards material relief, from observing how much the beauty of her sister rekindled the admiration of her former lover. Every five minutes seemed to be giving her more of his attention. He found her as handsome as she'd been last year; as good natured, and as unaffected.

When the gentlemen rose to go away, they were invited and engaged to dine at Longbourn in a few days time.

As soon as they were gone Elizabeth walked out to recover her spirits.

"Why, if he came only to be silent, grave, and indifferent," said she, "did he come at all? Teasing, teasing, man! I will think no more about him."

The following Tuesday a large party assembled at Longbourn; and the two, who were most anxiously expected, were in very good time. When they repaired to the dining-room, Elizabeth eagerly watched to see whether Bingley would take the place, which, in all their former parties, had belonged to him, by her sister. On entering the room, he seemed to hesitate, but Jane happened to look round and happened to smile; it was decided. He placed himself by her.

His behaviour to her sister was such, during dinner time, as showed an admiration of her, which persuaded Elizabeth, that if left wholly to himself, Jane's happiness and his own would be speedily secured. Mr. Darcy was on one side of her mother. She knew how little such a situation would give pleasure to either, or make either appear to advantage. She could see how seldom they spoke to each other and how formal and cold was their manner.

A few days after this visit, Mr. Bingley called again and alone. His friend had left him that morning for London, but was to return home in ten days time. Mrs. Bennet invited him to dine with them that evening and as he had no engagement her invitation was accepted with alacrity. He came in such very good time, the ladies were none of them were dressed. In ran Mrs. Bennet to her daughter's room in her dressing-gown.

"My dear Jane, make haste and hurry down. He's come. Mr. Bingley's come."

Jane would not be prevailed on to go downstairs without one of her sisters, so Mrs. Bennet's schemes for this day were ineffectual. But an engagement was formed chiefly through his own and Mrs. Bennet's means, for his coming next morning to shoot with her husband. Mr. Bingley and Mr. Bennet spent the morning together as had been agreed upon. Bingley, of course, returned with him to dinner and in the evening Mrs. Bennet's invitation was again at work to get everybody away from him and her daughter.

Elizabeth, on returning to the drawing-room perceived her sister and Bingley standing together as if engaged in earnest conversation. On seeing Elizabeth, Bingley whispered a few words to her sister and ran out of the room.

Jane could have no reserves from Elizabeth, and instantly embracing her, acknowledged, with the liveliest emotion, that she was the happiest creature in the world.

"I must go instantly to my mother," she cried. "I would not on any account trifle with her affectionate solicitude; or allow her to hear it from anyone but myself. He is gone to my father already. Oh! Lizzy, to know that what I have to relate will give such pleasure to all my dear family! how shall I bear so much happiness!"

Elizabeth now smiled at the rapidity and ease with which an affair was finally settled, that had given them so many previous months of suspense and vexation.

In a few minutes she was joined by Bingley. He shut the door and coming up to her claimed the good wishes and affection of a sister. Elizabeth honestly and heartily expressed her delight in the prospect of their relationship. They shook hands with great cordiality; and then she had to listen to all he had to say, of his own happiness, and of Jane's perfections.

One morning, about a week after Bingley's engagement with Jane had been formed, the family's attention was suddenly drawn to the window by the sound of a carriage. The horses were post; and neither the carriage, nor the livery of the servant who preceded it, were familiar to them. In a few minutes the door was thrown open, and their visitor entered. It was Lady Catherine de Bourgh.

She entered the room with an air more than usually ungracious, made no other reply to Elizabeth's salutation, than a slight inclination of the head, and sat down.

After a moment's silence she said very stiffly to Elizabeth,

"I hope you are well, Miss Bennet. That lady I suppose is your mother."

Elizabeth replied very concisely that she was.

"Miss Bennet, there seems to be a prettyish kind of a little wilderness on one side of your lawn. I should be glad to take a turn in it, if you will favour me with your company."

As soon as they entered the copse, Lady Catherine began in the following manner:-

"You can be at no loss, Miss Bennet, to understand the reason of my journey hither. Your own heart, your own conscience must tell you why I come."

"Indeed, you are mistaken, Madam. I have not been at all able to account for the honour of seeing you here."

"Miss Bennet," replied her ladyship in an angry tone, "you ought to know, that I am not to be trifled with. A report of a most alarming nature, reached me two days ago. I was told, that not only your sister was on the point of being most advantageously married, but that you, Miss Elizabeth Bennet, would, in all likelihood, be soon afterwards united to my nephew, Mr. Darcy. Do you not know that such a report is spread abroad?"

"I never heard that it was."

"And can you likewise declare that there is no foundation for it?"

"I do not pretend to possess equal frankness with your ladyship. You may ask questions, which I shall not choose to answer."

"This is not be borne. Miss Bennet, I insist on being satisfied. Has he, has my nephew, made you an offer of marriage? I am almost the nearest relation he has in the world, and as such entitled to know all his dearest concerns."

"But you are not entitled to know mine."

"This match can never take place. Mr. Darcy is engaged to my daughter. Now what have you to say?"

"Only this; that if he is so, you can have no reason to suppose he will make an offer to me."

Lady Catherine hesitated for a moment, and then replied.

"The engagement between them is of a peculiar kind. It was the favourite wish of his mother, as well as of mine. While in their cradles, we planned the union: do you pay no regard to the wishes of his friends?"

"I shall certainly not be kept from marrying your nephew, by knowing that his mother and aunt wished him to marry Miss de Bourgh."

"Miss Bennet, if you wilfully act against the inclinations of his family and friends you will be censured, slighted and despised, by everyone connected with him. You are to understand, Miss Bennet. I have not been used to submit to any person's whims. I have not been in the habit of brooking disappointment. My nephew and my daughter are formed for each other. If you were sensible for your own good you would not wish to quit the sphere, to which you have been brought up."

"In marrying your nephew, I should not consider myself as quitting that sphere. He is a gentleman; I am a gentleman's daughter."

"True. You are a gentleman's daughter. But who was your mother? Who are your uncles and aunts?"

"Whatever my connections may be," said Elizabeth "if your nephew does not object to them, they can be nothing to you."

"Tell me once and for all, are you engaged to him?"

Elizabeth could not but say after a moment's deliberation,

"I am not."

Lady Catherine seemed pleased.

"And will you promise me, never to enter into such an engagement?"

"I will make no promise of the kind."

"Miss Bennet, I am shocked and astonished. I shall not go away, until you have given me the assurance I require."

"And I certainly shall never give it. I must beg, therefore, to be importuned no farther on the subject."

"Not so hasty, if you please. What of your youngest sister's infamous elopement. I know it all; that the young man's marrying her was a patched-up business, the expense of your father and uncle. Is such a girl to be my nephew's sister? Are the shades of Pemberley to be thus polluted?"

"You can now have nothing further to say," Elizabeth resentfully answered. "You have insulted me in every possible method. I must beg to return to the house."

Her ladyship was highly incensed.

"Unfeeling, selfish girl. You are then resolved to have him. Very well, I shall know how to act. But depend upon it. It will carry my point. I take no leave of you, Miss Bennet. I send no compliments to your mother. You deserve no such attention. I am most seriously displeased."

Elizabeth made no answer and without attempting to persuade her ladyship to return to the house, walked quietly into it herself. She heard the carriage drive away as she proceeded upstairs. Her mother impatiently met her to ask why Lady Catherine would not come in again.

"She did not choose it," said her daughter, "she would go."

"I suppose she had nothing particular to say to you, Lizzy?"

Elizabeth was forced to give into a little falsehood here; for to acknowledge the substance of their conversation was impossible.

The next morning, as she was going downstairs, she was met by her father who came out of his library with a letter in his hand,

"Lizzy," said he, "I was going to look for you, come into my room. I have received a letter this morning that has astonished me exceedingly. I didn't know before that I had two daughters on the brink of matrimony. This letter is from Mr. Collins."

"From Mr. Collins? What can he have to say."

"He begins with a congratulations on the approaching nuptials of my eldest daughter, which seems he has been told by some of the good natured, gossiping Lucases. What relates to yourself is as follows. "Having thus offered you the sincere congratulations of Mrs. Collins and myself in this happy event, let me now add a short hint on the subject of another; your daughter Elizabeth, too, it is presumed, will not long bear the name of

Bennet and the chosen partner of her fate, may be reasonably looked up to, as one of the most illustrious personages in the land.

This young gentleman is blessed with splendid property, noble kindred, and extensive patronage. Yet in spite of all these temptations, let me warn my cousin Elizabeth, of what evil she may incur, with this gentleman's proposals. We have reason to imagine that his aunt, Lady Catherine de Bourgh, does not look on the match with a friendly eye."

"Mr. Darcy, you see, is the man! Now Lizzy, I think I have surprised you. Could he, or the Lucases, have pitched on any man, who would have given the lie more effectually to what they related?"

Elizabeth tried to join in her father's pleasantry, but could only force one most reluctant smile.

"Are you not diverted?"

"Oh!" cried Elizabeth, "I am exceedingly diverted, but it is so strange."

"Yes that is what makes it amusing. Had they fixed

on any other man it would have been nothing; but his perfect indifference, and your pointed dislike, make it so delightfully absurd!"

Elizabeth had never been more at a loss to make her feelings appear just what they were not. It was necessary to laugh, when she would rather have cried. Her father had most cruelly mortified her by what he said of Mr. Darcy's indifference. She could do nothing but wonder at such a want of penetration, or fear that perhaps, instead of his seeing too little, she might have fancied too much.

Mr. Bingley was able to bring Darcy with him to Longbourn before many days had passed after Lady Catherine's visit. Bingley, who wanted to be alone with Jane, proposed their all walking out. Mrs. Bennet was not in the habit of walking, Mary could never spare time, but the remaining five set off together. Bingley and Jane however, soon lagged behind. Elizabeth, Kitty and Darcy walked towards the Lucases, because Kitty wished to call upon Maria; and as Elizabeth saw no occasion for making it a general concern, when Kitty left them, she went boldly on with him alone.

While her courage was high she immediately said,

"Mr. Darcy, I can no longer help thanking you for your unexampled kindness to my poor sister. Were it known to the rest of the family I should not merely have my own gratitude to express."

"Oh, I'm sorry, exceedingly sorry," replied Darcy, in a tone of surprise and emotion, "that you have ever been informed of what may, in a mistaken light, have given you uneasiness. I didn't think Mrs. Gardiner was so little to be trusted."

"You must not blame my aunt. Lydia's thoughtlessness first betrayed to me that you had been concerned in the matter. Let me thank you again and again, in the name of all my family."

"If you will thank me," he replied, "let it be for yourself alone. Your family owe me nothing. Much as I respect them, I believe I thought only of you."

Elizabeth was too much embarrassed to say a word.

After a short pause, her companion added,

"You are too generous to trifle with me. If your feelings are still what they were last April, tell me so at once. My affections and wishes are unchanged, but one word from you will silence me on this matter forever."

Elizabeth forced herself to speak, not very fluently, but she gave him to understand that her sentiments had undergone so material a change, as to make her receive with gratitude and pleasure, his present assurances. He expressed himself on the occasion as sensibly and as warmly as a man violently in love can be supposed to do. Had Elizabeth been able to encounter his eye, she might have seen how well the expression of heart-felt delight, became him. But though she could not look she could listen. And he told her of his feelings which, in proving of what importance she was to him, made his affection every moment more valuable.

She learnt they were indebted for their present good understanding to the efforts of his aunt, Lady Catherine de Bourgh, who did call on him on her return through

London and there relate her journey to Longbourn, its motive, and the substance of her conversation with Elizabeth, unluckily for her ladyship, its effect had been exactly contrariwise.

"It taught me to hope," he said, "as I had scarcely ever allowed myself to hope before. I knew that, had you been irrevocably decided against me, you would have acknowledged it to Lady Catherine, frankly and openly."

Elizabeth coloured and laughed as she replied, "Yes, you know enough of my frankness to believe me capable of that. After abusing you so abominably to your face, I could have no scruple in abusing you to all your relations."

"What did you say of me, that I did not deserve?"

"Since then, we have both, I hope, improved in civilities," said Elizabeth.

"I cannot be so easily reconciled to myself. The recollection of what I then said, of my conduct, my manners, my expressions during the whole of it, is inexpressibly painful to me."

"You thought me devoid of ever a proper feeling, when you said I could neither have addressed you in any possible way that would induce you to accept me."

"Oh, do not repeat what I then said. I have long been most heartily ashamed of it."

Darcy mentioned his letter. "Did you on reading it give any credit to its contents?"

She explained what its effect on her had been and how gradually all her former prejudices had been removed.

"I was taught to be selfish and overbearing, to think meanly of all the rest of the world. And such I might still have been but for you dearest, loveliest Elizabeth. You showed me how insufficient were all my pretensions to please a woman worthy of being pleased."

"I am almost afraid of asking what you thought of me; when we met at Pemberley. You blamed me for coming?

"No indeed, I felt nothing but surprise."

"Your surprise could not be greater than mine. My conscience told me that I deserved no extraordinary politeness."

"My object then," replied Darcy, "was to show you, by every civility in my power, and hoped to lessen your ill opinion, by letting you see that your reproofs had been attended to. How soon any other wishes introduced themselves I can hardly tell, but believe in about half an hour after I had seen you."

He then told her of Georgiana's delight in her acquaintance, and her disappointment at its sudden interruption. After walking several miles in a leisurely manner, they found at last, on examining their watches, that it was time to go home. That night, she opened her heart to Jane.

"You are joking, Lizzy. This cannot be. Engaged to Mr. Darcy. No, no, you shall not deceive me. I know it to be impossible."

"I speak nothing but the truth. He still loves me and we are engaged."

"Good heavens! Can it be really so! Yet now I must believe you," cried Jane. "My dear Lizzy, I do congratulate you, but are you certain, forgive the question. Are you quite certain that you can be happy with him?"

"There can be no doubt of that, but are you pleased, Jane? Shall you like to have such a brother?"

"Oh, Lizzy! Do anything rather than marry without affection. Are you quite sure that you feel what you ought to do?"

She soon satisfied Jane by her solemn assurance of attachment. When convinced on that article, Jane had nothing farther to wish and half the night was spent in conversation.

During their walk the next day it was resolved that Mr. Bennet's consent should be asked in the course of the evening. Elizabeth reserved to herself the application of her mother's.

In the evening, soon after Mr. Bennet withdrew to the library, she saw Mr. Darcy rise also and follow him. When Mr. Darcy appeared again he approached the table where Elizabeth was sitting and said in a whisper, "Go to your father, he wants you in the library."

Her father was walking about the room looking grave and anxious.

"Lizzy," said he, "what are you doing? Are you out of your senses, to be accepting this man? Have you not always hated him?"

She assured him with some confusion of her attachment to Mr. Darcy.

"I do, I love him," she replied with tears in her eyes.

"Lizzy," said her father, "I have given him my consent. I now give it to you if you are resolved on having him. But let me advise you to think better of it. I know your disposition, Lizzy. I know you could be neither happy nor respectable unless you truly esteemed you husband."

Elizabeth, still more affected was earnest and solemn in her reply; and at length, by repeated assurance that Mr. Darcy was really the object of her choice, by explaining the gradual change which her estimation of him had undergone, and enumerating with energy all his good qualities, she did conquer her father's incredulity, and reconcile him to the match.

"Well, my dear," said he, when she ceased speaking, "I have no more to say. If this be the case, he deserves you."

To complete the favourable impression she then told him what Mr. Darcy had voluntarily done for Lydia. He heard her with astonishment.

"This is an evening of wonders, indeed! And so, Darcy did every thing. So much better. I shall offer to pay him tomorrow; he will rant and storm about his love for you, and there will be an end of the matter."

When her mother went up to her dressing-room that night, she followed her and made the important communication. Its effect was most extraordinary. For on first hearing it, Mrs. Bennet sat quite still unable to utter a syllable. She began at length to recover, to fidget about in her chair, get up, sit down again, wonder, and bless herself.

"Good gracious! Lord bless me! only think! Mr. Darcy! Who would have thought it! And is it really true? Oh! My dear Lizzy! Oh I am so pleased-so happy. Oh Lord! What will become of me. I shall go distracted."

Happy for all her maternal feeling was the day on which Mrs. Bennet got rid of her two deserving daughters. With what delighted pride she afterwards visited Mrs. Bingley and talked of Mrs. Darcy, may be guessed.

Mr. Bennet missed his second daughter exceedingly. His affection for her, drew him often to Pemberley especially when he was least expected. Mr. Bingley and Jane bought an estate in a neighbouring county to Derbyshire and Jane and Elizabeth in addition to every other source of happiness were within thirty miles of each other.

Wickham and Lydia, bore with philosophy the conviction that Elizabeth must now become acquainted with whatever of his ingratitude and falsehood had before been unknown to her; and in spite of everything, was not wholly without hope that Darcy might yet be prevailed on to make his fortune.

Though Darcy could never receive him at Pemberley, yet, for Elizabeth's sake, he assisted him further in his profession. Lydia was occasionally a visitor there when her husband was gone to enjoy himself in London or Bath.

Miss Bingley was very deeply mortified by Darcy's marriage but as she thought it advisable to retain the right of visiting at Pemberley, she dropped all her resentment, was fonder than ever of Georgiana, almost as attentive to Darcy as heretofore, and paid off every area of civility to Elizabeth.

Pemberley was now Georgiana's home; and the attachment of his sister and his wife was exactly what Darcy had hoped to see. Georgiana had the highest opinion in the world of Elizabeth; though at first she often listened with astonishment at her lively, sportive, manner of talking to her brother.

Lady Catherine was extremely indignant on the

marriage of her nephew; and as she gave way to all the genuine frankness of her character, for some time all intercourse was at an end. At length, her resentment gave way either to her affection for her nephew or her curiosity to see how his wife conducted herself. And she condescended to wait on them at Pemberley in spite of that pollution which its woods had received, not merely from the presence of such a mistress, but the visits of her uncle and aunt from the city.

With the Gardiners, they were always on the most intimate terms. Darcy, as well as Elizabeth, really loved them; and they were both ever sensible of the warmest gratitude toward the persons who, by bringing her into Derbyshire, had been the means of uniting them.